Eternal Guest

Novel

RUBÉN DAVID GONSALES GALLEGO

Wild Leaf, Inc. Chicago, Illinois

ISBN: 978-1-7361411-3-7
e-book ISBN: 978-1-7361411-4-4

Published in the United States by
Wild Leaf, Inc.
www.wildleafgroup.com

Translated from Russian: Rina Gallego
Edited by: Karina Riscos
Jacket design by: Natalia Kucherova
Jacket photographs: © Anne Yuyu

Manufactured in the United States of America

Books are available in quantity for promotional or premium use. For information on discounts and terms, please visit our website:
www.wildleafgroup.com

CONTENTS

To Polina and Michael Meltzer
who kept my body in working condition.

To Polina Meltzer
who compelled me to write this book.

To Polina Meltzer
who reminded me every day that I must write on that day.

The Beginning

I probably should not have written my third book. I am not exactly sure. I am not sure of the necessity to defend myself or to attack.

The only goal of my first book was to defend myself against being devoured by the outside world. The outside world, the world outside the gates of the orphanage, the gates of the nursing home, the boundaries of a country, the world I thought to be cruel and harsh—turned out to be not so cruel and harsh after all.

I did not believe that I had the strength to appear in front of the General Public once again, the carefree and accepting General Public, hungry for some genuine feelings. My second book did not go anywhere with the General Public. No matter. I made it on time. The royalties from my second book allowed me to buy my mother a cup of cappuccino and a bottle of Perrier water for one last time. I made it. This isn't much, but it isn't nothing. The second book should have been written before the first, but if it weren't for the urgency of my mother's cappuccino, it would have taken me a long time to write; a very long time. A usual bet in a rat race. The illness that one doesn't mention in casual conversation. The illness that overtakes the fastest and prostrates the strongest. What's left in my pocket? A couple of chips to play the roulette.

Oh well. A couple of extra chips can't hurt. One day this illness will conquer me. I am fine with that. But now it is my turn to conquer. My papers are in order, and the best medicine in the world is on my side. But the fear still sits inside me; the fear did not go anywhere. Fear of death. Fear of chemotherapy. Fear of losing for one last time.

Alexander

The name Alexander is common in Russia. Sasha.

He is crazy. A tall, intelligent man with a calm demeanor. As he entered the room, he did not demonstrate being surprised or ask any questions. He understood everything at once. Maybe it was because they studied my disability in the university. They must have studied my disability in the university.

"Why are you feeling awkward?"

A shy smile, an averted look.

"I am not feeling awkward; I am trying to formulate the problem."

"Formulate then."

"We just got into town, and I found a job via an advertisement. I passed the interview, and the job suits me. The advertisement said that the candidate needs to be familiar with the computer at the level of a system administrator."

"Congratulations."

"The problem is, I don't know how to use a computer."

"When do you start the job?"

"Tomorrow."

"It's all right, Sasha. My name is Ruben."

"I know. That's what I was told—you need to see Ruben."

"They were correct. What's your take?"

"I think that the computer can use its own fonts, and it can also use fonts that a human user drew. Can you teach me how to create fonts from scratch?"

"I can. But any publishing software has more than enough fonts. At first, you will need to learn how to use a computer. When was the last time you saw a computer?"

"In the university, at the mathematics department."

Okay. This guy is clearly not entirely alright in the head. If he is not a mathematician and has barely been around the computer, how does he intend to do his job?

"Okay, fine. Do you own a car?"

"I do. But it's small."

"Have you played sports?"

"A little."

"Do you know any foreign languages?"

"A little bit."

"So, you are Mister A Little Bit of Everything, right?"

"Right."

"What languages do you know?"

"Latin, English, French, Czech, Ukrainian... A bit of everything."

"This is getting weirder and weirder. How do you know Latin?"

"I am a doctor. But I don't practice."

"I understand that you don't practice. Times are wild. I thought doctors no longer have to study Latin."

"They don't; I did it out of curiosity."

"Good. Get your car over here, place me on the front seat. We are going for a little ride."

"I will return in half an hour."

The doctor knows how to transport a non-ambulant patient. The doctor doesn't need a block of instruction. His small Zaporozhetz rode confidently in a very un-Zaporozhetz-like high speed.

"Have you read Remarque?"

"I have. What exactly are you referring to?"

"*The Three Comrades.*"

"Thank you for the compliment."

"Have you replaced the engine?"

"Why bother? The car comes with an instruction booklet. If you do everything according to instructions, you can accomplish a lot, but folks rarely read instructions."

"Okay. Tomorrow you start the new job. Get yourself some tasks to do. But if they try to sit you behind the computer and start, tell them that it's your first day and you don't have administrative passwords yet."

"What happens the day after tomorrow?"

"You will have administrative passwords the day after tomorrow. Today, in the afternoon, ask for the office keys so you can remain behind after work, all computer specialists do that. Then come pick me up. We will have the night to install the anti-virus software and assign passwords to everyone. Can you sleep in breaks between work?"

"I suppose I could."

"Too many evasive answers. Have you ever had to go long without sleep?"

"I have. In the army. Can I ask you one last question?"

"Shoot."

"How much will I owe you?"

"A lot. And you will pay me in Czech krona."

"What the hell do you need Czech krona for, here?"

"Okay, zloty would also do fine. But krona is preferable. And not here, in Prague. You said you spoke Czech, didn't you?"

◆

There should be a chapter here about how they filmed a reality show. But there will be no such chapter. The author promised the readers to write of nothing but the triumph of the human spirit.

I abhor reality-shows. I abhor watching them and participating in them.

The reader is free to turn on the TV and watch any reality show to their liking. The reader won't miss anything, whether or not he or she watches the reality show.

◆

"Sasha, they are filming a documentary about me. A son looking for his mother."

"And does that make you happy or angry?"

"More happy than angry. What do you think of the plan to knock out the film crew and ask for political asylum in the Czech Republic or in Italy? You know Italian, don't you?"

"A little."

"You know a little Latin, so you know a little Italian. So, what about the film crew?"

"Nothing. No need to knock anyone out. I don't like to fight. If the necessity arises, the two of us will just get lost."

"Do you know the procedure for applying for political asylum?"

"A little."

Film

By way of clarification, I do not consider people with missing limbs to be disabled. I do not consider people who are blind or deaf from birth to be disabled either.

When people meet me for the first time, they look me in the eyes, and a million ways to help me goes through their minds. During the first five minutes of meeting someone, the calibration "friend-stranger" takes effect; people feel sorry for me. When I was young and brash, I got angry at them for it, and now I accept it with gratitude. The first five minutes of your conversation with someone are the most crucial five minutes of your entire relationship.

Life turned out this way. Things happened this way. The first people to have an intelligent conversation with me were doctors. Without Russian, Czech, Spanish, German, American, and Israeli doctors, my life had every chance of not happening.

Doctors are heroes obsessed with science, absolutely amazing people who sacrifice their youth and a piece of their own health to study medical books; the best people in the world. The importance of their contribution to the harmonious existence of humanity can only be compared with that of priests. One does not always manage to find a good priest or a good doctor. The best priests and the best doctors have a way of finding each other.

In my universe, in my vast imagined universe of a disabled man, a universe of dreams and hope, doctors are the best people in the world, and teachers are the smartest. The most beautiful girls in the world are TV reporters and radio hosts. Anyone can fall in love with a woman on TV, even the severely disabled. But you should never share these feelings with anyone. We can't even fall in love with nurses. The nurses are living, breathing women; they would laugh if were they to find out. They would most surely laugh.

Bad attendants don't count. Bad attendants have no gender. They are always cross and mean; they always wished to get rid of me. There were good attendants, but they were like grandmothers to us. I like the Russian word *babushka*—grandmother. It's a good word.

⸻ ◆ ⸻

The most necessary skill a disabled individual has to have, is understanding people. It's literally a life and death skill. If you haven't learned to understand people, you are dead. I learned.

⸻ ◆ ⸻

Sasha and I are in Prague. Prague is a beautiful city. They rolled my wheelchair into a café and told me: "Your mother is going to come. She will carry with her a hatchet or a bottle of acid. She will either hack you with a hatchet or pour acid into your face. But don't you worry, we will protect you."

A woman with a small, elegant handbag entered the café. The handbag wasn't large enough to carry a hatchet or a bottle of acid. She came up to me slowly.

A teacher. A bona fide teacher. I slowly inhaled to get enough air into my lungs. I didn't want to hurt anyone's feelings.

"You are being filmed with a hidden camera."

⸻ ◆ ⸻

"He is staying here. He is not going back to Russia."—my mother said.

And then a completely different film began.

The meeting

"You are being filmed with a hidden camera,"—I said.

"I thought so but thank you for trusting me enough to tell me that. You recognized me from the photo?"

"I didn't recognize, I realized. I realized that you are educated. In the orphanage, you don't have the luxury of focusing on one individual for a long time. There are exceptions, but..."

"I know. I grew up in an orphanage."

Aurora's voice is powerful and commanding. It is the voice of an individual who lives according to rules but can switch to a life with no rules, if need be. The voice from another world, a civilized world. The world is civilized, but not civilized enough to silence the voice of a girl from the orphanage.

We drink wine. Aurora's glass is empty. Nothing bad would have happened to a French woman even after a bottle of wine, but she forgets to drink. Aurora knows that Russian people drink a lot of alcohol when their emotions overwhelm them. She just keeps pouring the wine into my glass. I drink through a straw.

"You said that I am to stay here. But I am dying. My illness is incurable."

"Cancer?"

"No. Intestinal necrosis."

"I'm dying too. Third remission."

"Let's be dying together then."

We laugh. Orphanage graduates have a bizarre sense of humor.

"Can Sasha stay with you for a while?"—Aurora asks.

"Sasha can stay for as long as it takes. He wants to remain in the Czech Republic. Did you recognize me?"

"You look very much like your father. I recognized you the moment I saw you."

We are silent. Aurora tries hard not to cry. I don't cry.

Boys don't cry.

Pizza

That day, Aurora comes from work later than usual. She hangs up her trench-coat and comes up to me.

"Ruben, I feel bad."

"Something happened?"

"Not exactly, but I feel bad telling you what I am about to tell you."

"Tell me like it is. Your lab work came back bad?"

"No, not that. I came from work late, and I won't have time to cook dinner."

"We will die of hunger?"

Aurora is tired. I can see that she is so tired she doesn't even have the strength to smile.

"We are going to have to order pizza."

"Pizza is great. I have never seen pizza in my life. What's going to be on top?"

"Whatever you want."

"This can't be. What if I want pizza with sausage?"

"What type of sausage?"

"I don't know. Any sausage."

"Do you want BBQ chicken wings?"

"Instead of pizza?"

"Why instead? Sometimes when you order pizza, they offer you another course, for variety's sake."

The deliveryman brings us pizza. It is accompanied by BBQ chicken wings, but I decide to save the wings for tomorrow.

Now I realize why the intrepid Italian detectives and the cunning Italian Mafiosi order pizza at the tensest moments of the chase. They have no time to cook.

Aurora opens the box and takes the knife.

"Wait, Aurora, don't cut it yet. I want to look at the pizza a little more. It's so beautiful."

Show

"Ruben, we have been invited to a show,"—Aurora says—"they're promising to raise money to get you a wheelchair."

We fly. I love airports and large train terminals. I like watching people hurry along; I like watching trains leave, and planes take off. I like airports the best. You can dream in airports, and your dreams have no geographic limitations. Just blindly stick your finger into the globe and fly away. Of course, sticking your finger into the globe can land you someplace you don't want to be, or in the ocean altogether. No matter. If the first time doesn't work, there is always a second and a third. The main thing is to keep trying. The main thing is to believe that someone out there is waiting for you. The main thing is to know you will be needed someplace at once close and far away.

We flew into Spain as tourists. Being a tourist in Spain is nice enough and pleasant. Some charity loaned us a huge wheelchair. It was an abominable wheelchair, much worse than any of the wheelchairs I had in Russia.

A stage. They rolled me out onto the stage and asked me a couple of interesting questions. "Why do you need an electric wheelchair?" "What is the essence of your disability?"

The numbers representing the sum of donations shined on the electronic tableau behind me. With every one of my answers, the number kept rising. Yet another spastic attack contorted my body, and the uncomfortable wheelchair did not allow me to reposition myself. When I arched my back in an effort to reposition, my face was shown on screen close-up. The cameraman caught my face at the moment of maximum pain.

The cheerful host of the program jumped onstage and announced that the fundraising part was over. Some kind soul donated enough money to cover the cost of my wheelchair.

I wish health to this unknown woman who gave me this gift. I hope fortune smiles on her and her loved ones.

I also wish long years of life to the staff of that unknown charity. It took me several years to realize that they loaned me what passed for a standard wheelchair in Spain.

Toy soldiers

Explaining why knowing how to ski fast and shoot straight is valued more than knowing how to write good literature.

I have never understood, and will never understand, the logic of the powers that be. Maybe they are not humans right from birth. Perhaps they lose their human dignity at the pinnacle of power. I don't know. I'm not sure.

Everything was arranged in advance. Her Majesty Queen of Spain Sophia was told of my life. Her Majesty Queen Sophia has read excerpts from my book. It pleased Her Majesty to attend the sentimental opera performance of *Madame Butterfly,* and to meet me. It was all arranged in advance. The sentimental opera was supposed to evoke sentimental feelings in the queen.

For the first time in my life, I saw a reigning monarch up-close. The queen was magnificent! Her outfit was perfectly coordinated. All the jewelry found in Spain, anything that could be worn on fingers or hung from the neck, was worn, and hung.

We were introduced. Or, rather, I was introduced to the queen. I spoke all the fitting words from the pre-written text.

"He knows how to talk?"—asked the queen and left before anyone had a chance to answer her question.

It was all right. I expected nothing else. It is again my fault. My habitual boorishness and bad manners. I should have proven my loyalty to the Spanish crown with deeds, not with words. Two weeks before our meeting, a newly minted citizen of Spain was shown on TV. The King of Spain Juan Carlos I, granted Spanish citizenship to a German Olympic athlete, Johann Muhlegg. Spanish citizenship and 600 euro per month. May Heaven eternally smile on the kings and queens of Spain! I am guilty, and I won't deny it. Not only can I not ski, but I also doubt that I even have the strength to pull the trigger of a sports rifle. I never learned to cross-country-ski or to shoot.

◆

The Queen Sophia Museum. The museum, as usual, was nothing special. If I am invited, I go. I always agree to invitations. It turned out; I wasn't invited to look at the museum. I was invited to look at a ramp. It was evident that the ramp was constructed very hastily and very poorly. It was wooden; an awful piece of woodwork. My wheelchair had a powerful motor, but I was still apprehensive about riding up that ramp. I was told that the ramp was built especially for me. They thought I would feel flattered. I was anything but flattered, for it felt unpleasant to be the single person to use something useful. The sheer injustice of it angered me. Ramps have to be built for everyone, not just for celebrities. I am flattered by the attention paid to me as a celebrity but yearning for justice is stronger. All the goods in the world already go to the rich and famous. It's unfair to build a ramp just for me. It was also unfair that I was absolutely convinced that this ramp would not last long. I was told that it's a temporary ramp, built on the occasion of some anniversary. There is nothing more permanent in this world than temporary things.

There was nothing special about this museum. Photographs of kings and queens. Queen Sophia's family tree. No one would argue that it is better to be born rich than poor.

I liked the toy soldiers of Philip VI. They were intricately painted. They even had a miniature cannon.

Back in the faraway northern country where I was born, I did not have such beautiful toys. All of a sudden, I felt a yearning for a set of toy soldiers. I still don't why. Just because. I wanted to line the soldiers up on the floor, load the miniature cannon, and imagine my Spanish childhood that never happened.

"Aurora, buy me toy soldiers."

"I can't; they are expensive. You want me to buy you one soldier?"

"How much is one soldier?"

"Seventy euro."

"Forget it."

Mom and I walk along the museum corridors.

"Ruben, are you upset about not being able to buy a set of toy soldiers?"

"No. Not upset at all. I just imagined a little Spanish boy. No-one will ever buy him a set of royal toy soldiers. Nobody will buy him a cannon either. Russia doesn't have such a greedy king. A whole set of soldiers just for one individual. In the orphanage, parents of other children gave me toys sometimes. Not often, but they did. Why would I want toy soldiers or a toy cannon anyway? When I was a little boy, I had a tank. Almost a real tank, albeit a small one. A T-34."

Computer

I was often told that I have a computer inside my head. People didn't want to offend me. They merely wanted to say that I am very smart.

I lie on a mattress, on my stomach. It's comfortable. Aurora leaves for work.

"Do you need anything?"—she asks.

"A computer."

"Which computer in particular? Do you want to select one yourself?"

"Yes."

Sasha and I go to a store and buy a computer. Then we come home and install my hard drive on it. That's it. I won. I am no longer in Russia, and I have a computer.

Aurora comes home from work.

"I forgot to buy you keyboard stickers with Russian letters on them. A lot of work."

"It's okay; I learned to find my way around the keyboard. Let's order pizza tonight."

"You didn't like what I cooked yesterday?"

"It's not that. You know that I am almost indifferent about what to eat. Let's order pizza, and you will tell me all about Russian writers."

"I already told you."

"Tell me again. I will ask you questions, and you will answer, okay?"

"Okay"—Aurora smiles—"But what do you need Russian writers for? You have large gaps in your education. Want me to tell you about Gertrude Stein?"

"I do, but not tonight. Tonight, I've got me a computer."

We eat pizza. Aurora talks. She tells stories about a bunch of weird people who seem to drink vodka almost every waking moment. Russian writers drink vodka, get married, and divorce. What seems egregious to Aurora about their conduct seems absolutely ordinary to me. I glean the main point from Aurora's stories: they are human beings, regular, flawed human beings. They also have large gaps in their education. That's not the main thing. If they could become writers, so can I.

I am not very smart. Needless to say, there is no computer inside my head. I am simply alert and observant; it is essential, it is absolutely essential that I analyze everything that is going on around me. I am put in a position where I must plan for every contingency.

The Book

I lie on the mattress. It's comfortable for me to lie on a mattress. Two elbows are positioned on it securely. The bed is not as comfortable. When you are on a mattress, the whole apartment is yours. The bed is worse than a mattress. If you are in a bed, you are limited to the area of the bed, the small portions to the right and the left of the computer. I can get off the bed, but that means the computer has to be moved to the floor as well.

I lie on the mattress. No, the mattress is not really comfortable. It is, in fact, very uncomfortable, but it's not the mattress's fault. I rest my entire body weight on my right elbow. It is very uncomfortable. My right elbow hurts. My right elbow hurts really bad, but there is nothing I can do about it. I need my left hand for something else. From time to time, I place the body's weight on both elbows, but not for long. I rest. I can't afford to rest for long, though. If you relax, you lose. Pain can be withstood; I lived with pain all my life. When I realize the pain clouds my judgment, I roll onto my back and rest longer. Then I roll back onto my stomach. I try to convince myself that my right arm hurts less; I did rest, after all. I rest a long time, a very long time—about ten minutes. With the index finger of my left hand, I put my letters into the computer's memory. My white letters on a black background.

Aurora comes home from work. I press the Print button, and the printer spits out several pages.

I am used to the fact that Aurora's facial expression changes depending on the language she is speaking at this given moment. This time, Aurora speaks Russian to me as soon as she walks through the door, and the printer also spits out pages with Russian text. Aurora puts on her eyeglasses. I have never seen her like this. She reads carefully.

"You want me to print out everything? I have many more stories."

"Print *everything*,"—Aurora says with emphasis on the word everything, and I realize that now I am looking at Aurora as she arrives to work every day—focused and confident.

Aurora reads to herself. She neatly places pages from one stack to another. The stack of read pages grows steadily. I patiently wait for Aurora to finish.

"You liked it?"

"You see, Ruben. I can tell you everything about publishers and translators. You must learn to give interviews, hold your ground, and be invincible. This isn't a book everybody is going to like. It's funny to the point of being ridiculous. For half my life, I worked among writers, and now I don't even know what to do. I am a mother of a writer."

"You think I am a writer?"

"I am thinking of what to do about it"—Aurora looks me straight in the eye and I realize just how serious things are—"You are a Russian writer, but I don't know how to talk to the Russians. Without a publication in Russia, the Western literary establishment will not accept you."

Radio

Back in Russia, I loved listening to the American radio broadcasting in the Russian language. The teachers in school explained to us that foreign radio is nothing but lies. I agreed with the teachers. One program talked about how in the West, the disabled ride around town in battery-powered wheelchairs. What silly nonsense. Only toys work from batteries. I didn't even get mad at this radio station. I thought to myself—maybe it's science fiction they were broadcasting. I do love science fiction. When I read science fiction, I imagined myself to be a navigator of a spaceship or an alien with six tentacles. Six tentacles are much better than none at all.

My favorite American radio station was "Voice of America," because it regularly broadcast English lessons. English lessons on the radio are better than none at all. Much better.

Sergey

Sergey was my first editor.

Sergey is Aurora's ex-husband. Sergey is a Russian writer. Together they worked on Radio Liberty[1].

I thought that I was becoming a writer as I was reviewing his corrections of my text. I was mistaken. I became a writer the moment I got a short letter from him: *Ruben, your Volga story is one of the strongest descriptions of the Soviet hierarchy. I canceled all corrections. Sergey.*

Just like that. A writer must accept and reject corrections with equal lightness, at least at first glance.

The main thing is to never throw away the previous drafts.

---

[1] Radio Free Europe is a United States government-funded organization that report for countries where "the free flow of information is either banned by government authorities or not fully developed"

Limbus Press

Naum Nim offered my book to Konstantin Tublin. Just like that. The book quickly went into print.

Konstantin Tublin owns Limbus Press Publishers.

Naum Nim is the first man in Russia who saw something unique about my literary exercises. It also happens that he and I knew each other, personally, before my emigration.

These chaotic few lines just about describe the beginning of my literary career. I just lucked out.

When I am asked this constant nagging question, "how does one become a writer?" I already know that the asker does not want to hear the answer. What I am really being asked, is how to become a successful writer without actually doing anything. To that question, I have an absolutely honest and frank reply ready: "Become a doctor or a teacher, a pilot, or a submariner. Learn a skill, acquire a profession. Then, if you still have the desire to become a writer, become a writer. You have good chances. If there is no chance of acquiring a profession—no matter. Just write. Write and hope to be lucky. Maybe fortune will smile your way."

Teachers

Childhood. Russia. About every couple of years, I was moved from orphanage to orphanage. I liked going to school. School was an interesting game, an interesting game of life I liked to play.

The teacher entered the classroom, touched the blackboard, felt the teacher's desk and chair with his fingers. He sat down. The high school students already enlightened us on how to make him lose control of the classroom.

"Teacher,"—we asked—"Is it true that a German gouged your eyes out with a knife in a concentration camp?"

He got excited. His voice rose and fell.

"Not a German, a Nazi. Germans are the greatest composers. Nazism will end up in the garbage dump, and music will remain. Now you surely don't understand this, children. You will understand when you grow up."

The teacher left the classroom. He went to the teachers' lounge. He asked to be allowed to conduct a double lesson, two lessons of forty-five minutes. He didn't have to ask much. All the teachers knew that such request comes from him once a year and only in September. The math teacher gave his lesson up for this. He did so because he was sure that the music teacher would give up his lessons for him multiple times throughout the year. Mathematics is a serious subject and music—what's music, anyway? It's an auxiliary subject. It means nothing.

The teacher brought in a beautiful box. The box sported multiple buttons and two rolls of thin film.

"This is a tape recorder"—the teacher said—"They are not yet sold in our town. I went to Moscow just so I could buy it."

We waited for the music hesitantly, but we believed the teacher. One disk with a roll of film clearly had more music on it than dozens of the largest vinyl records. Clearly, you had to go all the way to Moscow to obtain such a miraculous device. Everyone knows that Moscow is the best city in the world.

The teacher carefully removed the blackboard from its frame and held the plug to the wall. The plug kept hitting the newly plastered wallpaper of our classroom. Every year they re-plastered the wallpaper. It was funny, but we tried not to laugh. It's wrong to laugh at one's own.

"As far as I understand, all the walking-able in this class use crutches. Gena is the only one who doesn't use crutches to walk."

Gena quickly rose from his chair.

"Sit down!"—the teacher spoke in a commanding voice, like a Soviet general in a movie.

Gena sat back down. Never again did we see our teacher be so strict.

The teacher took several objects out of his pocket. A small pocketknife, a pair of pliers, a roll of insulating tape. The teacher cut a neat circle into a thick layer of wallpaper, plastered one on top of another. There was no outlet under the wallpaper. We didn't laugh. In the orphanage, we didn't laugh at our own, even if they made mistakes. The teacher's pocket contained a new outlet.

The tape recorder played classical music. The music soared to the ceiling. Every time there was a pause in the music, the teacher would tell us about it. He gave explanations and put in a new tape with new music on it. After he was done with an explanation, he announced in a stern voice: "Any questions? No questions."

In his classroom, you didn't need to raise your hand to ask a question. Everyone could ask a question in his class. All you had to do was wait your turn and speak politely.

I had a question.

"Teacher, where did you learn to change outlets?"

"In a special school"

"A school for the blind?"

The teacher smiled. He must have been in a good mood that day.

"I learned in a regular special school. Shortly after the war, they were still around, but the country did not need so many special forces soldiers. I was fortunate to land old, experienced instructors. I was nineteen years old, but I was admitted. After the war, there were many people like me, without a profession, not knowing how to live a civilian life. We lived and breathed music. We studied almost 24/7. We didn't get enough sleep. We were so sleepy we weren't even hungry. The teachers would joke—"you didn't know the difference between day and night anyway; what did you need to sleep for?" Many were special forces vets, some of their operations were conducted at night, and they had to find their way around using their sense of touch."

That's it. That's how it worked. There would be no structured lesson. There would be no in-class assignments or homework. The teacher would just tell stories. It didn't matter which stories. It didn't matter at all.

"Many in my class drank themselves to oblivion; some departed this life. What use is a blind teacher to anyone? And what about me? I came to the school board to apply for a teaching job. I was told that they didn't have any jobs for me. So, I insisted that the board meet in full. While the board members were whispering to themselves, I drove two nails into the board, drew some lines, and started writing musical notes. The board members discussed the matter amongst themselves and decided that I am not to be allowed to teach. I was given a chance to say the last word. What could I say? I knew that reading sheet music is not taught in orphanages like yours, since the children can't play instruments due to their physical disabilities. I asked the board to enter what's written on the board in the minutes. Just as I suspected, there were no musicians among the board members. The board promised to enter what I wrote into the minutes, but they asked me to explain what the notes meant. And I wrote the first few cadences of the *L'Internationale*. I was going to take these notes to Moscow to appeal the decision of the board. The board didn't even discuss anything else. They entered into the minutes that, given my stellar ideological credentials, I am exactly the right individual to work with disabled children. They wrote many other flattering things as well. The board chairman gave me a long, firm handshake; everyone came up to me and congratulated me. *L'Internationale* is a special song - once written, it cannot be erased. That's how I got my job here."

He was a good teacher, a swell teacher. He never stepped on me when he encountered me in the hallway. He always bent down towards me and greeted me kindly.

And I so regretted not being born blind.

◆

The teacher entered the classroom. A regular teacher, nothing special about him.

He was fortunate enough to be born healthy. When he was nine years old, he saw that the small fry found an anti-tank mine. He was just passing by. He could have gone on his merry way. He could have called the grown-ups. He should have called the grown-ups. The anti-tank mine was too close to the road. Too close to the daycare center. The grown-ups were far away. Why would he need grown-ups anyway? He is not a baby; he is a grown man himself, nine years old, post-war generation. He chased the small fry away from the mine and sent them to call the grown-ups. The grown-ups would call in an EOD specialist. They would know what to do. Only before the grown-ups arrive, someone has to carry the mine away from the road. The last thing he remembers was carefully lifting it and starting towards the nearest ravine. He doesn't remember being transported to the hospital. It's just a contusion, some hearing loss for the rest of his life. He will live. The doctors didn't have the heart to tell him about his arms during the first wake-up. The arms had to be amputated.

The teacher told us about how, at university, he fell in love with a girl two years his senior. He passed all the tests required for a history teacher certification, and then he jumped two years up to be with his sweetheart and took all of the courses required to be a drawing and technical drafting teacher.

He told us how he created architectural drawings, holding the ruler to the drafting table with his lips. How he wasn't provided a drafting table during the final exams. How he was told that he is to take the final exam separately, so that his disability doesn't offend the normal students. How the instructor put a big running clock in front of him. You are on the clock now.

So what. No drafting table—no big deal. They haven't seen him do his homework. He placed a sheet of Whatman paper on the floor and held it down with books. And the most significant thing. Maybe that was the moment they realized—he won. He quickly removed his sweater. That's understandable. Nobody will be there to wipe his brow. He took off his shoes. Legs, arm stumps, teeth—everything was involved. He did not hear people's voices. He didn't hear them offering a drafting table—someone found an extra. His hearing loss had nothing to do with it. The world around him ceased to exist. It was just him and the draft. The only tool to defend his right to exist in this best of worlds.

The draft is ready. He went out to have a smoke. The head proctor came out to have a smoke with him. The head proctor gave him an expensive cigarette, and solicitously lit it.

"Are you happy now?"

"Excuse me, what was that?"

"We will check your draft, but I already know it won't have a single error. But I still don't understand why you did this. You should have approached this in a more conciliatory manner. You should have written an application mentioning how you heroically removed the mine and the disability you got from this. We could have given you a passing grade based on your previous work. Instead, you struck a heroic pose and set the whole pedagogical collective against yourself."

"Can I ask you a question?"

"Sure."

"I was passing by the hallway, and the other students appear to still be drafting. And if they draft wrong, they can re-test by law. They still have an hour and half, and my time is over. Don't get angry at me for asking."

"I am not angry. They have arms, don't you get it?"

I had excellent teachers. Not so bad, anyway. I am not getting angry; I understand. I write texts that are not so bad.

Socialism

Many years ago, a young girl from Paris, my mother, came to study in Moscow. She was sent to Moscow to study socialism. What nonsense is that. Whose bright idea was it to send a young girl far away from home, and what kind of socialism could she learn in Moscow, anyway? Life is cold and hungry in Moscow. In Moscow, people line up for food and clothes. Yes, Moscow is the world capital of socialism. Yes, compared to provincial Russia, Moscow is a paragon of happiness and prosperity. But to a girl from Paris, a winter in Moscow is a difficult ordeal. Why did Ignacio send his daughter to such a difficult faraway country?

It's not necessary to ask so many vague stupid questions. Ignacio Gallego was no fool. The answer is straightforward. Ignacio didn't pay a penny for his daughter's education in Moscow. He didn't have to pay for Aurora's food or lodging. And he didn't send her any money.

There is no need to demonize or idealize socialism. Socialism is a beautiful legend, and legends are immortal.

Money, just pure, simple money. Politics had nothing to do with it.

Kremlin

I was born in the Kremlin hospital. This hospital was very different from regular Russian hospitals. All the decisions in that hospital, including decisions on medical care, were made by people from the Central Committee of the Communist Party of the Union of Soviet Socialist Republics. These people were not doctors, but they were the highest power in the country. The Central Committee did not make life and death decisions. The Central Committee made all the decisions while essentially making none. Every medical procedure had to have the approval from the Central Committee before it could take place.

Aurora bore my sister, Anne, in a regular Russian obstetrics hospital. In a regular Russian obstetrics hospital, the doctor doesn't have to consult the Kremlin. In a regular Russian obstetrics hospital, the doctor himself makes decisions on medical care.

Prague

Prague is a beautiful city. If I were allowed, if it would have been possible, I would have never gone further than Prague. Why would I have wanted to?

But life is life. I found out everything I needed to find out. Many disabled people in the Czech Republic indeed moved around in electric wheelchairs. But a regular electric wheelchair did not suit me. I simply fell out of it. My custom-made wheelchair had to be assembled in Germany.

A Czech mechanic put together my first ever electric wheelchair. Yes, he had to design and assemble this wheelchair in Germany, but that's not the point. The Czech dreamt of creating wheelchairs for very disabled people, and I dreamt of a wheelchair.

It turns out we both dreamt of freedom.

Beauty

Beauty is a very amorphous notion. What's beautiful to me can be ugly to someone else. I am not a very handsome man, but if you ask my wife—she will tell you that none are handsomer. I am serious. I don't know just how handsome I am to Sophia, my daughter, but to her, I am the kindest and smartest father in the world. If she feels down and blue, she can always come up to daddy, take him by the index finger of his left hand, and hear that she is the prettiest and smartest little girl in the world.

I love Spain. Maybe it's because Spain is like Russia in so many ways. The people living in cruel, barbaric countries are capable of shining heroism that is impossible and unneeded in more civilized, almost perfectly run societies.

A hospital. A Spanish hospital. The ancient walls are covered with scary-looking crevices and bald spots. They put my bed in the hallway. To my left was a man from Mars. At least that's what he declared to the world and to the nurses rushing by. The man begged everyone to call six specific phone numbers. A doctor approaches him, patiently dials all six numbers, one after another, but the Universe is silent. The doctor promises that he will do his best to get in touch with Mars when he makes his next rounds.

The doctor comes up to me. I ask him why I was placed in the hallway. The nurse who is accompanying the doctor on his rounds gives me a kind, caring look. "Sir, it will take us time to run to the ward, and here you are in front of our eyes all the time. Such a young fellow. We are all very concerned about you." I understand she is not saying these things out of sheer politeness.

The pain twists me into an intricate pretzel, and I scream. I scream, and it feels like the ceiling is rotating above my face. Neither the doctor nor I have time to play the game of manners.

"Do you want to live?"—asks the doctor.

I have been living in Spain for a while, and I understand that this is a genuine question. What's the point of treating someone who doesn't want to live?

"I do,"—I reply and inhale more air to prepare for the next question.

"The surgery will have two parts. First, we will expose your intestines. There is nothing to be afraid of. Then, we will sew them back together, and you will have a normal digestive system."

"I am in pain"—I reply—"Do something."

"I'm sorry young man, you have to be patient until surgery. We must see the whole clinical picture, and this is impossible under anesthesia."

The doctor and Aurora step away. When Aurora returns, I can see that she did not "just sign a couple of papers," as she told me earlier.

"Ruben, the doctor says that in some cases, when the body does not receive enough nutrition, it begins digesting itself. He says you must have gone hungry a lot as a child. The X-ray shows necrosis all over your intestines, but the doctors suspect worse. They fear the necrosis spread to your other organs."

Aurora tries not to cry. I don't cry. Boys don't cry.

"Farewell. Thanks for everything,"—I tell Aurora.

The pain overwhelms me. My bed is rolled someplace. Lights. Large shining lights over the operating table. A woman in a surgical mask bends over me. Through the pain, I keep running my mouth: "A surgeon is no big deal. A surgeon just cuts and sews. Now the anesthesiologist—that's the thing. Anesthesiologists are the most beautiful women in the world. A woman anesthesiologist is bound to be beautiful, because she is the last thing a man sees before his death."

The anesthesiologist places a mask over my face and asks me to count to ten. I clearly remember saying "three." That's it. No more.

I wake up. The pain is gone. A fluffy cloud of calm and inner peace envelopes my brain that is not quite awake.

The doctor bends over me. He is happy; he cannot contain his excitement and elation.

"Hey. I performed surgeries like this in Colombia. In that country, your case is a regular occurrence. You are going to be just fine. Your liver and your kidneys are in order. The surgery went well. Of course, you will have to go on a diet. The diet is very strict. What will you eat as a favorite dish?"

The world around me is still in the mist of pleasant euphoria. Even this short conversation tired me, and the Spanish words slip through my fingers. I ask Aurora to translate from Russian.

"I will put a piece of meat in a pot of boiling water, and when the meat is almost cooked, I will add potatoes, cabbage, and beet. I will fry up some carrots and onions in the frying pan. I will add the contents of the frying pan to the broth in the pot. That's it."

I intentionally simplify the recipe because I am describing only what may be of interest to the doctor.

"Will you eat this often?"

"Often. Every day, most likely."

The doctor is trying not to offend me and maintain a neutral expression on his face, but he fails in that. He turns to a gaggle of residents and nurses accompanying him.

"He really will eat this every day"—one of the residents replies to the doctor's silent question out loud—"He is Russian. This dish is called borscht."

"Have you tried it?"

"I have. I was friends with a Russian girl"—he hesitates at the word "friends," but everyone understands him correctly.

"How does it taste?"

"Takes some getting used to. When you get used to it, it's perfectly edible."

The doctor smiles. He is happy with the explanation.

"Go on living, eat your borscht to your heart's content. Everything will be fine. You will have to be operated on in the future, about once every five years."

"What about the spasticity?"—I ask him.

"We took care of the spasticity in the lower part of your body. The seams won't come apart, don't sweat it. I just cut and sew, remember? The anesthesiologist will absolutely pay you a visit. You sang her praises before the sedation started working on you."

Piropos. At first glance, *piropos* are a simple compliment to a woman. But really, it's an art form, and it's highly prized in Spain. Books are published on how to compose *piropos, piropos* are made into musical and theatrical performances. *Piropos* from a book are not valued as highly as those composed on the spot. It's normal to expect a writer to come up with spontaneous *piropos*. If a man can't put a couple of words together in a woman's honor, he is not a man. If a writer can't express admiration for a woman, he is not a writer.

She walked in, a quick, confident gait, a slightly ironic smile.

"I am the anesthesiologist."

The sharp facial features reveal a woman of supreme confidence. A woman who knows her value and is used to giving instructions. Shoulder-length hair in small tight curls. Strong hands with a delicate manicure. I would never approach such a woman on the street. I would not have been able to gather the courage to even begin a conversation with her.

There is a TV set hanging above my bed. The sound is muted, but the female TV reporter looks straight into the camera and confidently addresses the viewers. She is beautiful.

"The most beautiful women in the world are movie stars and anesthesiologists,"—I blurt out.

She didn't respond in full strength. She realized I was still woozy after the surgery. But not answering at all would be impolite. A quick glance on the TV screen, a breezy smile to accompany a magnificent answer:

"Yes, TV reporters can be beautiful sometimes. But they are all made up."

A Bear

Madrid. Spanish cultural center. I speak Spanish reasonably well. I like everything. More than anything, I like those moments when the teacher is distracted from explaining Spanish grammar and starts to talk about himself, about the people and traditions of Spain. The Spanish live with an open heart. Living with an open-heart means living here and now.

The university cafeteria. A regular cafeteria. All the tables are occupied. That's understandable—it's a break between lectures.

"Ruben, come over to our table; it's fun times here."

A young man. A handsome youth. Aquiline nose, wavy shoulder-length hair. The young man teaches Spanish at the university. He uses his guitar to teach Spanish. The girls like caressing his hair; they like to learn Spanish by listening to his songs. And they like his guitar.

I navigate my wheelchair towards the table. Two tables are moved together. The young man is surrounded by beautiful girls and he is happy with himself. My skin is a shade or two darker than his; my wheelchair and my Russian accent preclude me from participating in the "who is the alpha?" contest. I greet everyone politely.

The young man is pleased with himself. He looks around at his girls. He is happy with this small victory. He shares a table with a famous writer.

"Want some beer, Ruben?"

"Sure thing."

"Too bad they only sell beer here. But I can run to the store and get you some vodka. I can bring you vodka. The Russians like their vodka, don't they?"

The girls giggle. They like the joke. The young man laughs too. Deep in my heart, I, too, laugh. I like the joke too. I am almost happy to be seen first as a writer, not as an invalid.

"No need to run anywhere. Beer will do just fine. You know, I keep vodka at home. Lots of it. I also have a set of matryoshka dolls and a bear with a balalaika. You know, he is a very smart bear. If he learned to play the balalaika, I am sure he can learn to play the guitar."

The girls are no longer giggling. The young man's bout of gaiety suddenly implodes. He realized that his joke about my Russian origins wasn't all that good. He doesn't know what to do. It really is not easy—to exit an awkward conversation and remain polite while doing it.

A good-looking middle-aged man approaches us. An elegant suit, graying hair, expensive eyeglasses, and the stern expression of a professor. Judging by the expression on his face, he is at once agitated and enraged.

The professor is exceedingly polite, and he is prepared for a very serious conversation. In a habitual gesture, the professor adjusts his eyeglasses.

"Señor Gallego. This young man is here on a temporary contract and doesn't have tenure. Regardless, I deeply regret what just happened. Please allow me to apologize to you on behalf of the university faculty."

Police Officer

I love Spain. I really do. Why wouldn't I love the place where my grandfather was born? If you take off your glasses, all the girls look happy, and all the boys look smart. A beautiful country, a charming royal couple, the best police officers. If you take off your glasses.

Eyeglasses come in different varieties. Way back when, many years ago, I believed that Spain was paradise on earth. Way back when I was naïve and stupid. Even now, I can be naïve and stupid sometimes. I would not give up my, at times, childish outlook on the world to anyone, for any amount of money. Let me be naïve. Let me be. A writer must remain a child in order to remain a writer. Let me be a simpleton looking at the world through rose colored glasses.

Aurora knew that she didn't have much time left because of that disease; the disease you don't say out loud. Aurora had a Spanish passport. I am her son, so I am entitled to Spanish citizenship. Everything is good; everything is legitimate.

The Spanish surgeon returned me to the world of the living, saved my life. He did everything he could have possibly done. A good surgeon. I respect surgeons. The doctor prescribed a strict diet for me and forbade me from traveling far away from the clinic. I obediently followed the doctor's instructions. I remained alive. I wanted to keep living.

But even such a beautiful country as Spain must have police officers. Me personally, I have nothing against police officers. Every state needs a police force. But it was in Spain where I had to confront the police head-on for the first time. The Spanish police were busily looking for me and did everything in their power not to find me.

They showed illegal immigrants on Spanish TV. Illegal immigrants were given blankets, food, and water. Illegal immigrants were given asylum. That was what was shown on TV. A good thing, TV is. Aurora and I watched TV often together. Then Aurora would turn on the news in her native French. The French journalists reported on how the Spanish authorities detained illegal immigrants and beat them within an inch of their lives. The French reporter didn't like an episode involving a young girl. The Spanish immigration agent put a black garbage bag over the girl's head. They put handcuffs on her wrists. But the girl didn't live to be deported. Her heart suddenly stopped. The dead don't sweat. The dead don't need water or food, or blankets. The dead need nothing.

I laid in bed on my stomach and ate soup. Just a regular soup.

My book was sold on every corner, and TV crews visited our residence on a weekly basis to film me. I gave interviews.

The soup was tasty. I ate the soup. Every human being must eat from time to time. I kept eating the soup and running away from the police. The police had everything they needed for a good hunt. I had nothing. The police had swift coast guard cutters, the police had automatic rifles, and even the most insignificant of police officers had a firearms holster. A firearms holster is not an accessory one wears for fashion.

I ate the soup. What harm could I have possibly caused by eating soup? I ate the soup, and the police officer rang my doorbell. Aurora went to open. Aurora was frightened. I, too, was frightened, but what choice did we have? My hands were too paralyzed to be placed behind my back and too thin to put in handcuffs. My legs were not strong enough to carry me away from the police. The police officer turned out to be a decent fellow. The police officers fumbled around on purpose while standing in the corridor leading to our apartment. He was trying to give me a chance. I am not Bruce Lee; I could not have kicked him while jumping on him from the top of the furniture. Funny as it sounds, I could not jump out the window either. The police officer waited, he waited long enough, he waited too long.

He entered. The handcuffs hung from his belt. He did not even have a baton. I don't know if he had a black garbage bag. I don't know, and I don't want to know. I had a choice—to run or to fight. Fine, let's fight. He was probably good at boxing. He carefully entered my room and stopped, maybe trying to guess my fighting tactic. Maybe he was figuring out the best way to knock the plate of soup from under my face, press my head to the bed, and cuff my hands behind my back. I don't know. I am not a police officer. The only thing that scared me was a bag over my head. As for broken collarbones, they can reset them in the nearest hospital.

"I am a police officer."

"I can see that. Please take a book from the shelf."

"I can't; I am a police officer."

"Please take the book from the shelf and compare the photograph on the cover to my face."

That he could do. He was trained to compare photographs to faces. Several times he switched his professional gaze from the book cover to my face and back. He compared the photograph again and again. He didn't know what to do. "I am a police officer,"—he kept repeating.

"I am compelled to place you under arrest."

"Please do. Just write in your protocol that I resisted. Write "actively resisted." Write that I beat you up. You can keep the book. It's a gift."

"No. I will give it to my supervisor. He has many books."

Airplane

Airports. I like railway terminals and airports. I like watching airplanes. The airplanes take off and touch down. I watch people depart and arrive. You can spend hours looking through huge windows of the airport building and imagine yourself choosing any plane you like and flying off to a destination of your choice. So many places where I have never been. So many places where I have arrived. I like trains as well. I really like trains, but I like airplanes much more. An airplane is capable of flying far away. It doesn't need a railway.

We are flying to Spain—Aurora, Anne, and me. We are returning from one temporary sojourn to another. We are flying from Rome to Madrid. I am a VIP who is returning from Italy. The Spanish like me; they like tourists and returning VIPs. The Spanish don't like poor people. They are right, probably. What use are the sick and the poor?

In a seat a little ahead of mine sits a handsome young man. An Italian. He is dressed very well. All the articles of clothing on him ideally suit his ideal figure. Immediately after landing, this young man opens a compact mirror and takes a comb out of his chest pocket. He adjusts his hairstyle and keeps looking in the mirror over and over again. I keep looking at the seats around him. What a strange mix of passengers. With the exception of this young man and me, the entire plane is occupied by young women all wearing the same sports uniform. The girls are coming back to Spain bearing silver medals. Silver medals in Olympic weightlifting is serious stuff.

A girl is sitting ahead of me. The chair is too small for her big powerful body. Her shoulders are massive and square, and her hair is rolled into a plain no-fuss bun. Her neighbor, a delicate figurine of a girl, tries to teach her friend a simple card game.

"You are so silly, Veronica. There are four suits in cards, and the ace outranks the king."

Veronica is not silly at all. Veronica honestly tries to keep her friend happy. I keep listening. The girls tease Veronica, one after another. It's easy; it's all too easy. Veronica is small among them; her task is to throw the discus. One has to train a lot to make it to the Olympic team. There is no way a silly person could win a silver medal. She is only a little girl among her older friends. A muscular girl and very kind to boot. A beautiful woman. Years of training gave her mountains of muscles, and the pressure to excel and rigorous schedules left cruel, bloody scars of stress on her. The stress left her with one single comfort—good, tasty food. What's so bad about a girl eating a lot anyway? Veronica must be heavy. Every kilogram of the discus thrower's weight serves as a counterweight to the discus. Veronica's friends tease her. Veronica admitted to having eaten a bar of chocolate before the competition.

"I am sorry"—I say in the confident voice of a mature man—"I like Veronica."

"But she eats too much chocolate"—someone objects in a childish voice.

They are children, nothing but children. They mean no harm. They are used to laughing at Veronica. Just used to it.

"But Veronica is kind and beautiful"—I insist—"When she buys chocolate, she shares it with everyone. And people leave their small children with her. She never refuses when someone needs her help."

Veronica turns to me in her chair. She blushes. It is obvious that she very rarely hears good things about herself.

"How did you know?"—Veronica asks.

"Know what?"

"That people leave their children with me."

"But I am right, am I not?"

"You are."

"Of course, he knows everything"—a girl in large eyeglasses says—"He is a writer."

Veronica's eyes shine. My compliment made her feel awkward and elated, all at once.

"I want to take a picture with you, Veronica. I will hang it on the wall in my room, and all the men in Spain will envy me."

"What about me, what about me?" -- I take a picture with every single one of these strong athletes.

I joke with everyone; I try my hardest. Every five minutes, I answer questions about airplanes and flight safety. What else can I do? Just to distract them for the next five minutes. It's been more than an hour, and our plane can't seem to take off. I notice the girls assiduously trying to hide the fact that they are frightened. I pretend not to notice how one or another goes to the tail end of the plane to make a phone call to her loved ones.

The pilot announces over the loudspeaker that our plane cannot take off due to an autopilot system malfunction.

The passengers are urgently evacuated. A heavy smell of kerosene lingers in the interior of the plane. An empty plane. The captain walks past empty armchairs and approaches us. He is cool, calm, and collected. The smell of kerosene turns stronger. The captain faces us calmly. The captain is always calm.

"Some strange autopilot you have in your plane. I never heard of autopilot running on kerosene."

"It was important to avoid panic. If you can, calm the girls down on a new plane."

"I will calm the girls down. Calming people down is my gift."

"Thank you."

Finally, we are loaded onto a different plane. The Spanish Olympic weightlifting team cautiously files into the plane. The Spanish Olympic weightlifting team is happy to see me, and the girls smile hesitantly.

"Veronica"—I call out—"Why do you think I gave you all these compliments?"

"Because you are a kind man."

"I am not a mean man, but we stopped at discussing that men are assholes and not to be believed, correct?"

Veronica smiles a little. A little is better than no smile at all; it's a very good result.

"Correct."

"They praise you, and then they use you."

"Yes."

"But I am a man too. Look here. I have a hard time sitting in a regular chair; I keep slipping down onto the floor. Can you seat me higher?"

Veronica approaches me, grabs me under the armpits, and seats me higher.

"Thank you,"—I tell Veronica—"I spoke to you for two hours just so I could ask you for help. Can you imagine what other men will do to get something more than that from you?"

"No. You are still not like the others. You are kind."

◆

The plane lands in Madrid. Anne runs to find out what's up with my wheelchair. Aurora and I remain onboard the plane.

A woman with a walkie-talkie and two bunches of keys on her belt enters the plane. Two sweet Spanish boys accompany her.

"Good day to you, señora."

The woman looks past me.

"Carry him away,"—she commands to the assistants.

"Excuse me, señora, where is Anne?"

"Your f...ing sister? She is running around the airport and demanding a stretcher."

"Is my wheelchair at the bottom of the airstair?

"Absolutely not. The standard wheelchair is at the bottom of the airstair."

"Excuse me, señora, but my son cannot use a standard wheelchair. He will fall out of it and break something,"—Aurora remarks politely.

"Shut up, you bitch."

Aurora cannot converse in this manner. She breaks into tears. Aurora is French; French violence is precise and refined. Civilized, refined, extraordinarily precise violence. On a side note, Aurora is not capable of any sort of violence. At least the French publisher robbed us clean without any consequences to themselves whatsoever.

"Take him,"—the woman commands.

The boys approach and politely ask how I wish to be carried. I ask them to bring a stretcher, equally politely.

"Did you hear what I told you? Carry him out of the plane at once!"

"But the señor doesn't wish to leave."

"Take him by force then."

The boys take a step back, they do not want to cause me pain.

Four years in the civilized world did rub off on me, somewhat. I am a kind, sweet and polite man. It is so easy—being charming and polite when your belly is full. But the thin veneer of civilization is just that—a veneer. The moment someone shows me aggression, they encounter an honest and straightforward Russian man from the Russian woods. I quickly arch my back and slip off the chair. Now I sit on the floor, my legs are not bent at the knee, and my back rests against the seat comfortably.

The woman bends over me and begins to scream in my face. I am about to find out many interesting things about my mother's and sister's origins as well as their moral character.

I don't scream. I slightly raise my voice, but I don't scream. I call this charming woman a fat stupid cow. I am comfortable having this exalted conversation in Spanish. Russian and Spanish languages share many curses in common. The great language of Byron and Shakespeare supplies one with four-letter words, but this word, unfortunately, is known internationally. In the end, I simply switch to Russian. I understand that the most innocent of phrases in an unknown language, seems like the darkest of curses to the uneducated.

The woman recoils from me. Her face turns crimson. Just for a second, for a split second, I feel sorry for her. Overweight people shouldn't exert themselves like this.

"What do you mean—he doesn't want?"—this not-so-intelligent woman screams at her aides.

She is wrong. Screaming at Spanish men is useless. More generally, screaming at anyone rarely makes sense. But the only woman who can scream at a Spanish man, is his mother.

Having failed to garner support from her aides, the woman switches back to me:

"You will leave, alright. I can call the police."

"Be my guest. At least the police have a stretcher. You might as well call in the army, the air force, and the navy. And I will call reporters."

At this point, I start rattling off the names of newspapers and TV stations.

A man comes out of the cockpit. He has been on duty for almost 24 hours. His voice is stern.

"What's going on here?"

"He doesn't want to leave the plane."

The woman answers the pilot solicitously. The pilot outranks her.

"Why don't you want to leave the plane? You like it here that much?"

The pilot doesn't raise his voice. He needs to prove nothing to no-one.

"I need a stretcher or my own wheelchair."

The man spoke quietly; everyone fell silent.

"This airplane belongs to an Italian airline, and Italian law governs here. The passenger's request is not unreasonable."

He turned around and went back to the cockpit.

Anne entered the plane. She had my wheelchair delivered straight to the bottom of the stairs.

"It's all right; I found the wheelchair. It was waiting for you right outside. The pilot helped. He spent this entire time arguing with the Spanish police on the phone."

The sweet Spanish boys carefully carry me out of the plane and place me in my wheelchair. I felt the joystick and slowly raised the back of the chair. Everything was fine. Two Spanish police officers were guarding my chair.

The woman with the keys informed the police officers that my mother is a saint, and my sister is an angel, a pure angel.

"I will see you to the exit. Will you go with me?"

"I will."

The woman quickly walked to the airport building. She almost ran. I followed her. We entered the elevator. I understand why she was in such a rush to get to the elevator. There is no eavesdropping equipment in the elevator. Elevators are not bugged, neither in her country nor in mine.

"Are you angry with me?"

"No, I am not."

"When you mentioned the press, I realized you looked a lot like Ruben Gallego. Will you file a complaint against me?"

"Listen"—I smiled in her face—"I am Ruben, and I will not complain about you. Can I ask you some questions?"

"Shoot."

"How much are the boys paid?"

"Six hundred Euro per month."

"And you?"

"Eight hundred."

"You have children?"

"Three of them."

The elevator stops. I glance around, trying to find Aurora and Anne, and press the joystick. I don't look back, I know. The woman wants to see me roll by the airport director's office with her own eyes. She didn't believe me. She believes no-one.

Citizenship

I am in Spain. Spain is a beautiful country. My books have been translated into several languages. My mother is Spanish. Everything is fine; everything should be fine. If my mother is Spanish—I, too, am Spanish. That should be clear to anyone.

A man who just moved to a strange country needs a lawyer.

"Ruben"—my lawyer tells me—"You have a problem. You were born in 1968. But children of Spanish mothers were not eligible for citizenship till 1974."

"Sounds bizarre. How are fathers superior to mothers? I understand that, historically, inheritance rights passed from father to child, but we are, after all, in the 21st century."

"You don't know Spanish history very well"—my lawyer tells me—"Not all ethnic groups in Spain passed ethnicity down from the father. Not all ethnic groups at all."

Okay, I may not be so well-versed in Spanish history, but I do know history. It's the truth. Not all ethnic groups pass ethnicity down from father. Not all ethnic groups at all.

———— ◆ ————

Time went on. My book kept being translated and published in more languages. Theoretically, I could have appealed to the king of Norway for help. Kings are kind people; they know and respect each other. Would it really be so difficult for the king of Norway to ask the king of Spain to bestow citizenship upon me?

———— ◆ ————

I don't want to launch into a description of a life of an illegal alien in a country with the best constitution in the world. I wish I could have regaled my readers with a story of how the brave Spanish policemen had me under surveillance day and night. I would have gladly told how the policemen looked for me but couldn't find me. I would have liked to write a long story with chases and gun battles. Of course, I would never have been able to fire a gun into someone in that long and beautiful story. The police officers' bullets would have whizzed by me but failed to hit me. The shepherds would have hidden me in the mountains, and the fishermen would not have surrendered me to the authorities for the largest of rewards. The only thing I could have done in this imaginary world—is to challenge the police to an honest battle. I would have put a shaving basin on my head; I would have mounted my faithful Rocinante, so that pikes could decide that I am truly worthy of Spanish citizenship.

Reality proved to be simpler and sadder. It wasn't the police officers who decided who should live and who should die. It wasn't the police officers who wished to get rid of me. Challenging a politician, any politician, to an honest battle is a senseless act.

Of course, I hid. I hid the best way I knew how. I hid by giving interviews to even the smallest Spanish newspapers. I hid by being on the radio. I hid by being on TV. It is complicated to get rid of someone who is on TV all the time.

When I began to write my first book, I decided not to write about sad things, if it can, at all, be avoided. Joyful things are harder to notice, but I give it a genuine elementary school try.

A miracle. A miracle happened. I failed to learn to ski or to shoot, but His Majesty King of Spain Juan Carlos I, bestowed Spanish citizenship upon me.

Under the law, I should have given an oath of allegiance to the king and the constitution in a great hall, under the Spanish flag. The great hall was on the second floor and inaccessible by wheelchair. I had to give my oath in a small corridor across from a Coke vending machine. I sincerely swore not to overthrow the Spanish government.

Everything was fine. Just one thought worries me. The Coke vending machine was broken. My oath of loyalty to the Spanish crown given in front of a broken American Coke vending machine—is it valid?

I am not sure, and there is no-one I can ask. For myself, I resolved never to overthrow the Spanish government. Just in case.

United States of America

The United States of America. It's a country in North America. It was called different things at different times, but now it is called that.

Very recently, about three hundred years ago, there was no such country. People were living on the land, yes, but there was no country. Just like in every young country, everything was brand-new, hastily cobbled together, everyone united—even though everyone has his own legend—everyone united under the flag, the national anthem, and the apple pie. Stuffed chicken the size of a turkey, a turkey the size of a suckling pig, and pigs...you ought to see the pigs in this country. They are the size of a cow. If the pigs are so large, one can only imagine how large the cows are.

The tallest skyscrapers in the world, the largest airplanes, the largest bridges, and the largest waterfalls. The country of the large and of the magnificent. The country of Hollywood dreams. The country of Oz. The country of hope. The country of harsh reality.

People. What people are there! People in the United States of America are very diverse. Never before in my life have, I seen so many different people at one time.

The United States of America greeted me with nothing, gave me nothing—neither good nor bad. A strange, cold country. The United States of America is a great country. It's a great country for the young and the hardworking, and I proved to be unworthy of that greatness. According to American standards, I am neither young nor strong. I have nothing to give to America. America owes me nothing in return.

The United States of America is a warm and hospitable country, but I proved unworthy of that warmth and that hospitality.

The United States of America is a country for the strong and the smart, but I proved to be neither strong nor smart.

The United States of America refuses no-one the right to be. Every immigrant has a right to wash dishes in a restaurant. Every American has a right to mow someone else's lawn. Everyone has a right, but I am not everyone. I am too weak and too lazy to work construction. I am incapable of washing dishes.

The United States of America has done much for the rights of the disabled. But I am not just disabled. I am also married. Okay, a married, disabled man is no longer considered disabled. A married, disabled man needs no help.

A married, disabled man has every right to stick a barrel of the gun in his mouth. A married, disabled man does not need to pretend and beg. If his wife is the real deal, she will follow her husband to Valhalla.

It's an immense privilege, almost a fairy tale. If only the hands were working, if only there was an opportunity to position the gun barrel across from the mouth.

I was unlucky. My wife proved to be far from the real deal. Rina did not spare me the bullet before last.

I do not judge her—everyone has a right to live. But bills are bills. Bills have to be paid regardless. If you can't pay your bills -- then be so kind as to kill all your dependents and follow them to the grave. Leave honorably, like one is supposed to leave if he or she cannot pay his or her bills. Leave without babbling about liberty and justice for all.

We had a daughter. We had a defective daughter. Oh well. The only solution to most problems is to write checks. The annual salary of an attorney for the US government was barely enough to cover three months of professional help for Sophia.

The United States of America is a great country. I am not joking; I am absolutely serious. In all the civilized world, a disabled individual has no right to government help, if he or she happens to be married.

Oh well. I have lived a long life, indeed a very long life by Russian standards. I wrote books and essays that will be read and studied for generations to come. It's time to go. I want to die. I was sick of dying, but it was necessary. I was hoping that Israel will not allow a single mother with a disabled child to drown. I knew that in Israel, autism doesn't surprise anyone.

I didn't die. I have the best daughter in the world. I am married, but my marital status has no bearing on my eligibility for disability assistance. I am married, but it doesn't occur to anyone in this country to deny Sophia the right to an education because her father moves around in an electric wheelchair. I know I am repeating myself, but I have no compunction about repeating the truth. Sophia, my little, non-verbal autistic Sophia, invented her own way of greeting me—she touches my hand. Sophia decided on her own, what to do if the world proves overwhelming and complicated. She comes up to me and buries her face in my left shoulder. I hug Sophia, and we do not need to explain anything to anyone.

Good-bye, USA; hello, Israel.

Polina

Sixteen years. For sixteen years, I haven't lived in Russia. Strange as it may sound, I have never felt nostalgia. Maybe this phenomenon really exists; maybe emigrants themselves designated it as a sickness in the moments of a personal crisis of despair. I don't know. Stumbling and falling, withstanding blow after blow, I never considered missing the country of my birth. Not once.

You came suddenly. You came like so many others. People come and go, each with his or her own pain, each with his or her own unique burden. We spoke some. We talked of nothing, or, rather, I talked of nonsense. I talked and talked non-stop, trying to fill gaps in our mutual silence.

The little girl inside you didn't cry. She was used to not crying in front of strangers. The girl sat silently in a chair, desperately trying to push small mouthfuls of hot tea through her throat and further inside. The girl held on, trying to mask the pain she was it, to mask the desire to hide, to bury oneself, to exchange the forced politeness of human interaction for ten minutes free of pain. Just ten minutes. She refused to accept compromise from fate, and if one is to be perfectly fair and truthful, fate had no solutions—radical, compromises, or otherwise. Just pain. Constant unbearable pain. Pain and diagnosis, which nobody wants to talk about. The pain of a little girl and her thirst for life.

Neither the pain nor the diagnosis kept us from having a conversation that evening. We talked about books. *Der Steppenwolf* and *Red Laughter*. Your favorite books and mine. Their titles became our passwords. Book titles were a code, a password in Russia that I have left. Book titles retained that function in Russia that you left.

For sixteen years, I haven't been to Russia. Sixteen years is not even a quarter of a century.

TV, media, the internet—a senseless flood of information. Who in their right mind would look for information in newspapers, be they "fresh" or from sixteen years ago? Only in books.

Very few people risk coming back, having seen me once. You have come back. You had your own nostalgia.

Barzilai Hospital

Israel. Hospitals. Hospitals come in all shapes and sizes. Hospitals, however good or bad they may be, are not meant to house disabled patients. It seems counter-intuitive. Where, if not in the hospital, would there be professionals who understand the challenges of living paralyzed? In reality, things are much more straightforward. A paralyzed individual has to be turned in bed every couple of hours. Who is going to do it? Any hospital, however good, always lacks enough nursing staff. No hospital is capable of providing one-on-one care. Life and death are on schedule. The clock started ticking.

It happened in the pharmacy. The man screamed. The man shouted at the top of his lungs. He came to the pharmacy to complain about not being summoned to his fourth chemotherapy appointment. He was called several times at home in his own native language, which happened to be Russian. He was also mailed a written reminder.

"Okay, I know you called me, but why were your initial calls and letters in Hebrew?"

I looked at his hair and nails. The hair was slightly graying. I looked at him and rejoiced for him, the way I rejoice every time an elderly person succeeds in something. I knew everything there is to know about the disease that nobody wants to talk about. Aurora held out for eight years until cancer returned with a vengeance. Every day of these eight years, she was afraid it would come back.

The man screamed loudly, and the very professional pharmacy staff managed to calm him down. He was given a referral written in Russian. Victory! He went to his fourth chemotherapy appointment, clutching the hard-won referral in his hand. He went being confident in his rights. He went, and I remembered Aurora. He went to the right chemotherapy appointment, and even his hair was all right. He went at the right time and in the right mood. He went, and the pharmacy staff rejoiced for him.

They knew that the outcome of chemotherapy often depends on the patient's mood and disposition.

Scream, scream to your heart's content. Scream away at the top of your healthy lungs. Scream without hesitation and use all resources of your almost healthy body. I will rejoice to hear you scream the same way the pharmacy staff rejoices, the same way the hospital staff will rejoice.

——— ◆ ———

It was no accident that I ended up in the hospital. My time has come. I have squeezed out of my body seven more years than the Spanish surgeon predicted. This time the anesthesiologist was male. I am no expert in male beauty. I was just overjoyed that he spoke Spanish. It so happened that the Spanish language is my talisman to remain in the world of the living. I felt queasy, my head was spinning, but the doctor would not let me go to the world of dreams and phantoms just yet. "Talk to me just a little more,"—he asked me in Spanish. "Where are you from?"—I asked him. "Colombia,"—replied the doctor. I conscientiously counted to three, and the world for me was no more.

Polina reclined the back of my chair and made use of this for a bed. She pretended to be asleep. I, having lost my place in the world between dreams and reality, kept calling to her. In my dreams, I flew through space, ascended mountains, and descended to the bottom of the ocean. But in space and underwater, I kept looking for Polina. Powerful medicines kept propelling my spaceship further and further into space. At every stop, I called for Polina.

"No, don't touch me"—I plead—"Polina will come right back; she just went out to have a smoke."

The Jewish doctors performed a miracle. They just cut things inside me and sewed them back together. For a long time, they cut, and they sewed. An ordinary miracle. A surgery with little chance of success.

The Jewish doctors did not ask me whether I wanted to live or not. A silly question; everyone knows life is priceless. I am not a very strong individual; I fell into despair and fell asleep. Polina was in my dreams, and she was there the moment I woke up. I remembered what Polina's answer was to my question, "Why do you bother?". She replied with a phrase from a Russian film, "One lives not for joy, one lives for integrity."

I wished to die. Polina didn't want to let me go. She read out loud to me; she read Fowles. I remember her saying, "We don't know what awaits us *there*." When I turned into a patient from hell in the bouts of ICU delirium, I knew that I would see Polina. I had no right to have doubts; I had no right to think of death. I had no right to reset to zero what Fowles wrote for me. I had no right to fail them, Fowles or Polina.

Six months after the surgery, Polina gave me half a glass of orange juice. I haven't had orange juice for more than fifteen years. In small sips, I savored the tastiest juice in the world from Polina's hands. The juice was indeed delicious, but I would not have brought myself to try it without Polina. I would have chickened out.

My body has been repaired. I have been given a new lease on life; my expiration date just moved fifty years into the future. And why not? People live to be a hundred years old. I will not argue or seek to prove anything to anyone. Barzilai is the best hospital in the best country in the world. I live!

Dream

On occasion, I walk in my dreams. Even in my dreams, I don't know how to do it correctly. When a Czech mechanic built the first electric wheelchair for me, I started flying in my dreams. It wasn't a flight like how a bird flies. Rather, I glide above the surface of the earth. When I just started using a wheelchair, I found it next to impossible to have a conversation with a person walking beside me. Navigating the wheelchair demanded full concentration.

I knew you would come. I knew we would talk. I just got unaccustomed to having a conversation. I forgot what it's like—to have a conversation.

We walked along the sidewalk, and I can't say I understood everything you said. You kept saying words from intelligent books, and I just felt joy. It's been a while since I heard those words. I just rejoiced, without worry or fear. Only now, I tried to convince myself, to console myself, and finally believe. In that second, when I saw you in my dream, walking along with the wheelchair, I didn't believe it. I didn't believe myself; I didn't believe in myself. I still don't.

Morning. A regular morning. People get up early to go to work. People rush going about their daily lives. You have come. We sit home, just the two of us. We just sit and talk. You get up to give me a glass of water. It's just a glass of regular water, nothing special. You almost bring the glass to my lips.

Suddenly you cave in. You slowly take a knee and prostrate yourself on the floor. Strange as it may sound, you carefully place the glass next to yourself. I know this feeling of boundless pain, pain so intense it clouds one's vision. I understand your urge to focus on the glass. At the moment of pain, it is essential to focus on a thought or an object. A simple glass will do, but it's much better to fearlessly reach out for a prayer or any quote from The Book.

You lay on your back. I am puzzled as to what to do next but try not to show it.

"You lucked out today. You have the best coach in the Olympic sport of crawling on one's back. Let's begin. We smile, we bend our left leg—and push! We bend our right leg—and push!"

I understand that you would give anything now not to hear my voice. You are in pain, in a great deal of pain. But I also know that if you don't take a painkiller, things will get worse, much worse. I try not to think about this "worse."

"You are at the finish line. I know that you can't see very well right now. Lift your arm. The table has three drawers. There is a bag in the middle drawer. Good, very good."

I name the medicines, even though I know full well that you are a much bigger expert in medicines than I am. I overdo it in the safety department. You hold the bag with medicines close to your face and select the needed one. You see poorly, but you still see. That's good. You remembered the location where you placed a glass of water. That is also good.

Half an hour later, we sit in the kitchen and have tea. Everything is fine; nothing happened. Everything is fine.

Cucumbers

You are slicing cucumbers. I watch the knife pause hesitantly before every motion. I realize. This is metastasis. If the unmentionable disease starts affecting the eyes, that's it. This isn't just a quick onset of total blindness. It also means death. What could be worse than death? Only a protracted and torturous agony. I am afraid. I just met you recently, and I haven't gotten to know you enough. I am terrified. We just met, and now you need to leave. Leave for eternity. Your illness and your quick death are unavoidable. So young and beautiful, you still have to die. I am convinced death has caught up with you quietly. Death will come at the wrong time. It always does.

I suggest you see an eye doctor. I tell you that you need new glasses. You don't agree right away. You don't like doctors. The glasses you have are pretty and fashionable. I suggest again and again.

We go to the eye doctor together. You select the most beautiful frames. Back in the faraway northern country, they prescribed you glasses that made it impossible to function. These glasses, like fragments of a crooked mirror, distorted your world. I compliment the new frames. Again, and again, I praise the glasses made in Israel.

You are slicing a cucumber. Neat circles of a sliced cucumber are carefully spread on the cutting board. I rejoice. I tell you that I love cucumbers.

You are slicing the cucumber into neat rings. It's only a delay. It's only a step on the way. It's cucumbers, just cucumbers.

Wife

We use too many words. Way too many. An abundance of words. The more frequently we use a word, the less it means. What does the phrase "I have a good watch," mean? I don't know, and no-one knows. A watch is a watch. A watch shows time, and that's that. If a man has a watch, he just has a watch, nothing more, nothing less. A watch is a tool for telling time. Knowing what time it is, is very important.

Adjectives are even worse. What does the word "white" mean? What is it for? White, whiter, the whitest. I realize it's just an advertisement for laundry powder, but I am completely lost when I hear that this is the only place where you can find white. It's actually possible for people to believe that one can go to a store, buy the same laundry powder as twenty years ago, and the sheets will be whiter than they were yesterday. A year ago, white shirts were not as white; all the colors in the rainbow blended together in white, not as white as a million years ago. We are used to it. For too long, we have been persuaded, we gave up, and now we agree with everything we are being told. White is whiter this year than last year. Wooden furniture became more wooden, and my metal pan has more metal in it than it did last year.

There are too many words, way too many. I don't need so many. I don't need the chaos of meaningless words and phrases. White should mean white, wooden should mean wooden, and I should mean me. I want to delve into the original sense of simple words, I really do.

What does the word "good" mean? Nobody can give a precise definition. Good means good. To every individual human being, "good watch," "good snow," or "good frying pan" means something different, and that itself is good.

A little soldier with an M-16 rifle in her hands and wearing a regulation-prescribed uniform. A vast desert surrounds the soldier, and countless miles separate her from her home. The soldier is just one tiny point in the chaos of a relentless and endless world. In this cold, cruel world, people kill each other, and they are not bothered by abstract philosophical discussions. Military propaganda doesn't care much for selecting the right epithet. White bandages in the war are anything but white, so why bother pretending otherwise.

The cloudless sky breathes death. The sweltering desert breathes cold, calculated murder. An automatic rifle that smart engineers created for quick and effective extermination of a unique and priceless gift—a human life. For more than ten years, this picture has been the desktop background for every one of personal computers. The computers broke down, the programs malfunctioned, but this picture will remain with me for as long as I live. I intend to live long. At least the Israeli doctor promised me a long and happy life.

She found me on the world-wide-web. She didn't know what to do with her life next. A soldier, a small soldier, who conscientiously follows orders and is absolutely lost in the unpredictable vortex of peaceful civilian life. In the army, they taught her everything they teach someone who faces death every day. They taught her everything she needed to die well.

After we married, Rina had to learn to live, not to survive. She knew very well what she needed to do to honorably take her place in a wooden box covered with a stares-and-stripes flag of the world's greatest country. She was taught to kill and to die. Civilian life felt like an unattainable mirage. They taught her to be ready for death every day and to look for the most effective way to kill herself.

I did not wish to marry. I went through two divorces. I had my fill of family life, and I realized that my disability causes nothing but pain and suffering to those around me. I could not marry and did not want to bring any more of this to anyone.

We frequently spoke on the phone for hours on end. Words meant nothing. "Fine"—I said—"If we don't work out, if you realize that I am not what you need—what will you do?" "Wait up, Ruben"—Rina replied—"I need to check the calendar." Rina found the calendar, and several dates into the future were marked with opportunities to volunteer to deploy to Afghanistan. "If things don't work out between us, my plan B is to go on a deployment to Afghanistan,"—Rina said. There was no pathos or coquetry in this phrase. Afghanistan it is. They can kill her in Afghanistan, and nothing is more beautiful than death for your country.

Rina dreamed of a flag over the coffin, of her fellow soldiers saluting into the air, she dreamed of a beautiful funeral ceremony. After all, we are all mortal, but not everyone suffers the bitter misfortune of being seriously injured, get an errant piece of shrapnel, or a bullet that was meant for you. Losing your legs is not the end of the world. People live without legs. But some injuries are much worse.

It's normal to dream of death. Many soldiers do. Brave soldiers are ready to give every minute of their life to their profession. Soldiers can talk of anything, but no-one wants to come home blind or completely paralyzed. In America, they write books and film movies about veterans, including disabled veterans. These books and movies are all about duty, honor, country. But the Hollywood movies always leave the disabled veteran an opportunity to move his hands. Or at least one hand.

We are together. We live together well. I am married. I have a good wife.

Rina

A girl. Just a little girl. My desktop will have always had a picture of a little girl. She is holding a rifle. How would the rifle help her in the middle of a vast desert? There is no magazine in the rifle, but even a loaded rifle would not help her if she stepped on a landmine. In the army, children grow differently than in the civilian life. The military is a big warm family of boys and girls. The army takes someone as a child, and when a soldier is killed, he forever remains eighteen or twenty years old. The words "army" and "death" are often mentioned together. It's good when they are.

But sometimes, the war takes someone out of the world of the living slowly, in several bites. I am not talking about "disability-lite." Not having legs is "disability-lite." Not having arms is "disability-lite." In the case of a light disability, the army does its utmost to care for the individual. The army is honest, as honest as can be. And then, after the United States Army did everything it had the power to do to help a disabled veteran, he is transitioned to the civilian life, and that's when the horror starts. Free soup kitchens work round the clock, free homeless shelters degrade you to the point of inhumanity, and a free meal gives a few moments of warmth to someone now considered worthless and useless. So many free things suddenly happen in a country where everything is measured in a dollar equivalent.

The huge country allocated a small burial plot to my little soldier. A free plot on the Arlington cemetery.

"Ruben, does it upset you that we lost our Arlington cemetery burial plot?"

"No, it does not."

I can be woken up in the middle of the night—and answer any questions, solve any mathematical problem. I remember everything. They told us in school: "You must answer any question out of the school curriculum even if someone wakes you up in the middle of the night." We were taught well. Good schools with good teachers were located in a provincial backwater far from Moscow. The further from Moscow, the better.

We speak on the phone. It's evening in Texas while it's deep into the night in Germany.

"Ruben, I nearly broke a friend's arm today. We haven't seen each other for a long time. He squeezed my hand in a painful handshake, and I twisted his arm back."

"Is this a friend from Russia?"

"Yes. How did you know?"

"It's something Russian men do. They squeeze a woman's hand in a handshake to make her scream in pain."

"Yes. He was just trying to joke, but I was trained to react quickly. He doubled over in pain, and I just stood there apologizing."

"You didn't slam his head against the wall?"

"Why would I do that? He was in pain already."

"To avenge for other women."

"It didn't occur to me."

"Then everything is fine. What's the problem?"

"Ruben."

"Yes?"

"It's not about him; it's about me. I did this on autopilot. How am I going to manage in civilian life?"

"You will manage just fine. I can't imagine an American who would joke like this. And if someone touches you without being invited, feel free to slam them into the wall."

"You don't understand. I don't want to beat up anyone."

"I understand. You are a product of the army, and I am the product of an orphanage. Do you know how many guys from our orphanage graduated straight to prison? It was funny sometimes. A guy with a missing arm was charged with using excessive force. Four guys attacked him, and he has only one arm. The cops laughed that they had no place to handcuffs on. This guy had to be handcuffed to the police officer. You can put handcuffs on a legless man, but then you would have to carry him in your arms."

"What am I to do?"

"Nothing. Just live. Just try to remain alive with a full complement of your legs and arms."

"You do realize that I am not bragging?"

"I do. I understand. Forget it happened. It will pass on. Time will pass, and you will forget everything. You will forget."

Family. The one alike to God

A youth wearing glasses. Just a youth wearing glasses. A nose with a light bump, a slight stoop in his back. I met his kind in Russia. Rarely, but I did. Way too rarely. Thanks be to God of Abraham, Isaac, and Jacob, there is plenty of such people in the country I live in now. They come in different varieties—from teenagers to grown men. Grown men who know their value. Real men.

I am an orphan. According to the official paperwork, I have very few relatives. What's the use in relatives you did not select for yourself anyway? What's the use in relatives who are appointed to you by the Central Committee of the Communist Party of Spain? The Central Committee and I have nothing to do with one another.

Being born an orphan is truly a stroke of good luck. Some of my schoolmates were visited by relatives. The weeping women tried to feed their biological relative in one day for the 365 days of the year ahead, 366 on leap years. It made no sense in the orphanage. It's much cooler to wait for the relatives to leave and then apportion the food fair and square with your classmates, have a feast of sweetmeats and tea from a glass jar.

It so happened that I never got to choose. It so happened that my schoolmates were closer to me than my blood relatives from Central America or Western Europe. And sometimes the person's profession determines who their relatives are. Your relatives are your fellow Olympic athletes or mountaineers, or submariners. Relatives such as these do not need to be schooled on the basics of life; they will never ask dumb questions requiring equally dumb answers.

A youth, just a youth wearing glasses. A functional young man from a functional family. Michael, the one alike to God. He entered and glanced around the room. I was familiar with that glance; we had no need to discuss functional families or functional orphanages. He simply became part of my family.

Family. Dennis

I am an orphan. To put it simpler, I have no relatives. From a purely biological standpoint, I have more than enough relatives. Several dozen on my mother's side and about a hundred on my father's. But that's only from a purely biological standpoint. If I were a purebred dog, I would be under obligation to have blood relatives. But I am not a dog. I am free to pick my own relatives.

In Russia, Dennis was a Scout, and not just any Scout—a Scout leader. Once a Scout, always a Scout.

Here, in Israel, Dennis fought in a war. He never talks about it. He does talk about his service, though. When he does, he tells a slightly different story every time. Based on Dennis's stories, his army service was limited to getting drunk and telling his chain of command to go fuck themselves. Based on Dennis's stories, army service is nothing but entertainment and having nothing to do. Dennis is fibbing and doesn't even hide it. If you insist, Dennis will tell you about a minor injury. A minor injury, a mere trifle. If you insist, you will see a sort of razor-sharp focus in Dennis's eyes. I have seen it before, in the eyes of WWII veterans. If a man can't or won't talk about combat—that is his right. You should not pry or insist. He will tell when he is ready, whenever that might be.

When I need an urgent doctor's visit and an urgent referral, Dennis finds these for me, quietly and casually. We are very different people, Dennis, and me. We enjoy a calm, steady friendship. He knows I am there for him, and I know he is there for me. That's important.

Dennis is giving Sophia a haircut. He is calm, absolutely calm. Sophia arches her back and screams. While Michael and Polina restrain Sophia, Dennis calmly and confidently aims his electric hair clipper at her scalp—a second here, a half a second there. It is a tough proposition, giving Sophia a haircut.

We live in the same neighborhood and don't meet very often. When I swam in the sea for the first time in my life—Dennis was there. When I entered a jacuzzi for the first time in my life—Dennis was there. When

I took my first underwater dive to look at tropical fish—Dennis was there.

I was born into this world an orphan. So what? I have a unique opportunity to decide who will be my family.

Potatoes

American movies are the best movies in the world. No-one would argue with that. The USA is a vast country. From sea to shining sea, millions of people are united by the movies, American movies, common to all fifty states. It comes in very handy. If you want to understand an American, all you have to do is find a relevant movie to watch with him or her.

Rina is an American soldier. Forever. No matter what happens to her in the future, I am convinced that her army service will always be her best and brightest memory.

Regardless of where he is stationed and for how long, every American soldier knows a girl is waiting for him at home. His parents and friends are also waiting for him. Mom, dad, grandma, and grandpa wait for Johnny to come marching home again. Sometimes a soldier doesn't have a grandpa. Sometimes a soldier doesn't have a dad; it happens. But mom and grandma will always be there waiting. There may or may not be a girl. Not every girl would agree to wait for the soldier. Not every girl would agree to see the soldier off to war. Not every girl would agree to smile mechanically at her friends and relatives every day. Not every girl can cry into her pillow every night and promise herself that she will wait for the hero to come home. To wait and to promise herself that she will accept the soldier after the war regardless of the shape in which he returns—blind, or with missing arms, or with missing legs. She will accept him, knowing that blindness or missing limbs is not the worst thing that can happen to a soldier in a war. She will accept him even if he returns from war a different human being, even if he has trouble recognizing her when they meet again.

Very often, a soldier knows that no girl is waiting for him at home.

No girl? No biggie. There is a beautiful American movie about that too. The soldier brings a girl home from war. She is lovely and strong. Like him, she hates war. Only at first glance, she seems timid and frail. But the fire of war is forever imprinted on the retina of her beautiful eyes, just like it is on the retina of the soldier's eyes. They will accept each other just like that. The people who have not been in a war will not understand them. They won't understand. So what, no biggie.

An American soldier is a real deal. He will buy his girl anything she asks. The girl will ask him if she can select anything from the supermarket shelf, and he will smile awkwardly. To him, this is just a provincial supermarket. Nothing special. Of course, she can buy anything she wants. She can buy a whole turkey, a giant chocolate cake. He will pay; of course, he will. He will buy her a new cellphone with the best plan. He is a soldier. If he said he would buy—he will. He is prepared to stroll along the supermarket shelves with her, picking the best there is in the world.

But the girl doesn't need to stroll. The girl knows what ultimate happiness is. She loads a humongous bag of rice onto the supermarket cart.

"Ruben, is there anything else you want?"—Rina cautiously interrupts the flow of images in my head.

"No. I was just thinking about the movie we watched. I haven't lived in Russia for a while. I am a famous writer. Why would we possibly need a humongous bag of potatoes?"

We laugh. We are at ease together. We understand each other.

"Ruben, we are not in any hurry."

"Everything is fine, really."

"You have been staring at this bag of potatoes for quite some time. Are you sure you want to buy it?"

"No, I am not. But let's get another five pounds of potatoes."

Rina doesn't argue. She loads a five-pound pack of potatoes onto the supermarket cart. The package bears a proud notation *Grown and packed in Idaho.*

Potatoes are the real deal. Potatoes can be made into latkes. Potatoes can be home fried. Fried potatoes are the best dish in the world. Google produces more than five hundred potatoes recipe for one search inquiry. Potatoes can be boiled in their skin and eaten with nothing but salt.

Potatoes are real food, nothing like rice. Ask any Russian from Moscow or St. Petersburg. Ask any American. Ask any Idahoan.

His Land, Tajikistan

I love museums. Museums come in all shapes and sizes. Sometimes they exhibit paintings and sometimes artifacts. I can stare at pictures and artifacts for hours on end. Sometimes one can glimpse the movement of the human soul in an inanimate object. Sometimes—and it usually is so—the time allocated to each visitor is not nearly enough.

Inanimate objects in the museum reveal motion. The motion brings me joy, awakens my imagination, and brings to light something very personal. Personal to each visitor. Time should stop in museums. That's why museums exist in the first place. Motion in motionless, static in dynamic. An ordinary miracle—a man looks at an object and lives its entire life in a span of an hour or so. Everything is real in museums. Just like in real life. Not enough time to stop and think.

And sometimes, an extraordinary miracle occurs in a museum. Sometimes the museum curator can reveal more in ten minutes than the contents of his entire exhibition hall.

Rina and I are in the museum. Rina thinks I should leave the house more often to look at Israel's museums and its natural beauty. Sometimes I agree with Rina. Of course, both museums and nature can be seen on the computer screen. Why leave the room if all exhibits of all museums in the world are accessible to the modern man in two clicks of the computer mouse.

It's midday. A wonderful time when the only people present in the museum are employees.

The museum employee hears us conversing in Russian and approaches us.

"Where are you from?"

"It's hard to explain."

I load onto this elderly man volumes and volumes of my intricate biography. I realize that he understands maybe a half of what I am telling him. I am a grandson of Spaniards, son of a Frenchwoman, husband of a Jewish woman. And a miracle happens. My vis-à-vis tells me about his life, cramming everything important into ten minutes. What can be told in a span of ten minutes.

He is an old man. He had everything in the country he left behind—a wife, children, a two-story house, and a car. And then a miracle happened in his life. A small, shabby car stopped at the broad intersection. The light changed to green, and the car continued standing, blocking traffic. East is east. The driver was just finishing his lunch. A police officer approached the car and asked the driver why he isn't driving forward. "Why are you standing there, blocking traffic?"—asked the officer. The driver replied quietly, firmly, and respectfully: "I am a Tadjik, and this is my land, Tajikistan. I stop and go as I please."

My vis-à-vis, the museum curator, had a bigger and faster car than this Tadjik man. A beautiful wife, a well-appointed house, what else does a man need? The same day he went to the synagogue and asked the rabbi:

"Rabbi, where is my land? I am okay with not having a rich house, I can walk and not have a car, but I want to walk on my own land."

In two weeks, he gathered all the necessary paperwork. For two weeks, he tried to convince his wife to join him. It took him two weeks to bid farewell to the land that wasn't his. Now he is retired. Here in Israel, he welcomed his wife into a new home and helped her fight the disease, which one does not name out loud. Here in Israel, he buried a woman who declined to jump off the cliff and fly with him many years before. Here in Israel, he loved and was loved. A new family, many children. Here in Israel, he had trouble naming all his grandsons and granddaughters for me.

"Have you settled in Israel permanently?"—this elderly man asked me.

"I have,"—I replied.

"Do you know that a miracle can happen to you here? If the Big Boss Upstairs wills it, you will get off your wheelchair and walk with your own legs?"

"I had a better choice. I could either sit in the wheelchair, decline slowly, and live not long, or I could risk my life going onto the operating table and then sit in the wheelchair and look at the sun of Israel, at the land of Israel, at the museums of Israel."

We wished each other health and long years. East is east.

I am a Jew

I am a Jew. Israel is a big country. Israel's state languages are Hebrew and Arabic.

India too is a big country. So is Russia. If I meet an Indian, I will tell him he is Indian. If that's a mistake—no big deal. Everyone has a right to make a mistake. I am deeply convinced that every resident of India is an Indian. I may be mistaken. After all, many residents of India don't consider themselves Indian. It is a man's right to consider himself what he wants. More than a billion Indians are separated by ethnicity, religion, and caste. So what? Whether they like it or not, they are Indian.

Politeness and innate curiosity can drive me to ask which ethnicity and which caste is my vis-à-vis from. I will write down his place in a complex hierarchy of ethnicities, castes, and languages in my handy little handbook.

No, not really. Even in this text, I try to be precise and not let the tight collar of political correctness interfere with that precision.

Even here, in my own head and in the silicone world of computer memory, I try to be as politically correct as I possibly can.

I sincerely hope that my reader will forgive me this moment of weakness and a sudden bout of political correctness.

If fate brings me to sit at the same table as Brahmin, I will eat what a Brahmin eats.

If fate brings me to sit at the same table as a Dalit, I will eat what a Dalit eats, as long as I can be sure that the food was thoroughly cooked through. I will only drink water. I will bring water with me. More likely, I will bring Coca Cola in a nice-looking bottle. I am sure even Dalits have heard of this carbonated drink from the United States of America.

If they refuse to drink Coca Cola, I will understand. In any case, no-one is under any obligation to eat what I eat or to drink Coca-Cola.

Without separating people into races and castes, I still harbor a healthy respect for those who love their land.

The Indians don't much like the English language, but it's the only lingua franca in which different ethnic groups in India can communicate. An Indian can like or not like England, but he will speak Oxford English if he wants to amount to anything in life.

Syria and Iraq, Lebanon, and Jordan—all these countries to me are countries of the Arabic language. A small trickle of news from those countries does not satisfy my immense curiosity.

I never followed the steps of Lawrence of Arabia through the desert.

I like the countries of the East. They will always remain a mystery to me, and I like solving riddles. I have never been there, and I will never be. In my pocket, I have the passport of the State of Israel. I will be killed. I will be killed for having Israeli citizenship. Even the passport of a US citizen will not save me in this case. More than four hundred fifty million people consider me a Jew because I live in Israel.

So, a Jew it will be. I didn't choose this. They chose for me.

When a rocket fragment misses my house, I know that this fragment was meant for me. The people who launched the rocket wanted the fragment to tear into me. In any place and any time, murderers will find me and detonate an explosive next to me. They don't care which blood flows through my veins. They want me dead. They call me a Jew. So, a Jew it's going to be.

Way back then when I traveled around the world nobody wanted to listen to my explanations. I was a Russian to everyone.

I know that there are people who are well integrated into the country where they immigrated. They speak the local language fluently; they wear what the locals wear and look every bit local. These people are embarrassed to call themselves Russian. I don't understand. For my entire life outside of Russia, I responded to the question "Where are you from?" with the words "I am Russian." I realize full well that if I call myself "Russian," I bear full responsibility for Russia's questionable political decisions. But by calling myself Russian, I also let my vis-à-vis know that space exploration, Russian ballet, and Russian poetry are also a source of pride for me.

Now, that I live in a multiethnic country called Israel, everyone is calling me a Jew. Everyone, from Japan to the good old US of A. Even the UN, the most fair and progressive organization, routinely passes resolutions against the Jews. The UN is a supremely politically correct organization. Therefore, from the top of the mountain of useless paperwork, time and time again, Jews are being asked to give up a little more. I am confident that good and decent people work for the UN. I agree to read all the paperwork written against me. All I am required to do—is admit to being an Israeli. We are being asked nothing, a mere trifle, really. I must give the Golan Heights to the friendly neighbors. Of course, the peaceful neighbors will never roll out their long-range artillery onto the Golan Heights.

The unfortunate Arabs that I oppress will fire a rocket into me, into my small wheelchair. No! I forgot! They won't be able to fire into me! The UN resolutions will stand between them and me, like a veritable Iron Dome. The UN resolutions will fearlessly rush into battle. The UN resolutions will protect the young and the old in the State of Israel.

Random fragments of rockets will strike their targets. Random rocket launches will aim at me, a peaceful Jew. Everything will be fine. Everything will be like the UN wants. It will be without me. But until that happens, I will be Jew. At home and during trips abroad, I will not replace the truth with politically correct euphemisms. I am a Jew. I chose this land.

Edward

Very often, noble deeds are interpreted as a consequence of a man's religious choice. The description of good character qualities can begin with religious dogma and end with religious dogma. Evil deeds are reduced to atheism and lack of belief in the supernatural.

While I concede an advantage of faith over agnosticism, I can't ignore fundamental questions. For example, why there are more religious people in the world than decent people.

Lucky for me, there are folks who, while proclaiming themselves atheists, perform deeds comparable to deeds of believers, the best and brightest of them. These people have developed their own ethical code. Such people who try to behave their best every second of their lives cause me to feel admiration.

Aurora. Aurora was like this. Everything for others, nothing for herself. Aurora helped those around her without a hint of compensation. Aurora departed this world, not leaving a cent behind. Edward, I don't think you will have a chance to get fabulously wealthy. You once had lots of money, and you were good at making money. Polina and I are very close; I don't know why. It could be magic or genes, or upbringing. You will probably find this amusing.

It sometimes happened that people recognized Aurora's style as they were reading my text. Edward. I continually learn about you from Polina. The fact that you took care of your old relatives (and not all of them were blood relatives)—is a worthy choice of a strong individual. Your conduct towards your son touches me deeply, and I have seen many things in life. We have never met personally, but I am convinced that I have known you for at least three years. I see you clearly in Polina: abrupt, confident, and very kind.

Live long, Edward. Many people in this world need you. I need you.

Ho Chi Min

Wu Tu Hien. A normal, common Vietnamese name.

"Call me Hien. Or Ivan. When I lived in Russia, they called me Ivan."

Ivan. I smile. Of course, Ivan. A small and wiry wisp of a man coiled into a spring. Very polite, very gracious, very courteous. A little too polite. One of the guys, Ivan, Vanya. How many times did you change your name, Hien? How many times did lay in wait, aim, and strike? How many times did you change your passport, your political party, or your entire life? How many times did you kill? How many times did you "neutralize" your rivals?

You are strong and agile, and you are smart and cunning. Only once you miscalculated, only once. That mistake was enough to teach you a lesson for the rest of your life. You trust no-one and no-one trusts you. No wife, no children, no friends, no relatives. No-one. Just a prolonged fight. Just patient waiting. Just hate for those who came after Ho Chi Min.

"That son of a bitch Ho Chi Min. We slept on the same straw mat. I made rice for him. We shared rice sitting on a straw mat in a prison cell. We ate together, waited for the sentence together. He betrayed me. You say *Ho Chi Min*, and I understand you."

"Hien, will you have Chinese food?"

"In Vietnam, we eat anything that moves, except a wheel."

We order Chinese takeout. The deliveryman brings us food, lots of food. I know, Hien, that you cannot eat a lot, but the very sight of abundant food is pleasing to your eyes. We start eating—Aurora, Anne, and I. Hien feels for the table surface to the right of his plate. Chopsticks! Anne and Aurora know how to use chopsticks. Everyone knows how to use chopsticks in these modern days. Hien takes a fork into his right hand and assiduously tries to grab a piece of meat with it. I nod to Anne and roll my eyes in Hien's direction. Anne quickly places the missing pair of chopsticks in front of Hien.

"How old are you, Hien?"

"Seventy-two."

"When we met four years ago, you were seventy-two as well."

"If you know the answer, why do you ask?"

"But age is really nothing. You are a man, Hien. Why would a man want to hide his age?"

"My age doesn't change because I am waiting."

"Waiting for what?"

"His death. You know, Ruben, I can still move around a lot. Every day I conduct physical fitness. Did I say this right in Russian—*conduct physical fitness*?"

"How many hours do you conduct physical fitness every day?

"Six hours. I am an old man; I can't do exercises for a long time. So, I just four hours in the morning and two at night."

"In Russian, this is called *training*."

"I know. That's a special Vietnamese type of training. But I like the words "conduct physical fitness." When I am no longer able to move, I will sit in the room quietly and slowly sip chicken broth. They wait. Slowly they wait for their enemy to die. I know some comrades who have been sipping chicken broth for many years now. If a man wills it, he can live to a hundred years old."

"I read about some people living to be a hundred and forty, but I don't believe it."

"I have met people who have been a hundred and forty for a while. Do you believe me?

"You I believe."

Hien smiles happily. He eats quickly. Bending low over the plate, he shoves pieces of meat into his mouth. He can enjoy the side dish later if no-one takes the plate away from him.

"Hien, have some chicken; we have plenty of chicken."

"Thank you."

Hien places half of a chicken onto his plate. I have never seen a man wield two pairs of chopsticks at once. Hien tries to eat slowly, but old habits die hard.

"Hien, why are you in such a hurry? Once a man ate the food, it cannot be taken out of his stomach; it's impossible."

"It's very possible."

Hien is in a good mood. I can see how food changes even his appearance.

“Before coming to visit you, I haven’t eaten for two days.”

“You couldn’t afford food?”

“I wanted to be prepared for a fight. Fighting is better on an empty stomach. If I had to fight right now, I would have regurgitated the food. If the loser has food in his stomach, he can be forced to regurgitate it, and the winner can eat it. Food is strength. Blood of your enemy is strength.”

Anne leaves the room. This conversation is clearly too much for her.

“Hien, when did you stop being on edge?”

“When I entered your home.”

“Why didn’t you want to eat in a restaurant? Because enemies could have been there?”

Hien is happy. Hien is smiling.

“Enemies could have been anywhere.”

“Hien, tell me about the Americans. Have you seen the movie *Apocalypse Now*?

“Everyone asks about the Americans. It’s an okay movie.”

“But the Americans used napalm.”

“It’s a silly toy.”

“I don’t get it. I really don’t. It must be horrible—when a human being turns into a torch.”

“Look”—Hien takes a knee, and I can clearly see an imaginary weapon in his hands. He moves lightly and flawlessly, and I realize that this is a part of his “physical fitness” regimen and that he just shed forty years in a matter of moments—“One, two, three. You fire three shots into the knee of each. Then you take out those who run to help the wounded one by one. Twenty people just like that. I ran away while they were unwinding their hose full of napalm.”

“But the Americans abandoned their own in the jungle.”

“Americans are normal people. I like Americans.”

“Hien, why don’t you write a book of your own. You must have a lot to share. Like you shared food with Ho Chi Min, for example.”

“Nobody will read my book. But that’s not the main thing. Imagine, I shared rice with Ho Chi Min, I brewed tea for him, and he put me in prison. Where do I get words to describe this? Your book is so joyful. You are a kind man. In prison, they would have strangled you in no time.”

“Why me?”

"Because you are a kind man. You see only the good in people. You feel sorry for everyone, even the dog. You are a kind man, just like Prishvin. I translated Prishvin from Russian to Vietnamese. You strangled no-one at night, and in your book, no-one is strangled at night. Prishvin didn't eat the dog, and neither did you."

"You are a translator?"

"No."

"But you translated books."

"I did many things in life. I am not greedy. One man was sitting in our prison cell, the head honcho. But the head honcho doesn't have the luxury to be greedy. They strangled him slightly at night, then they released him and strangled him again. This continued all night. It was the night before the morning of a big holiday. In the morning, they gave us meat for breakfast. Three small pieces of meat. He took his piece, and the chopsticks stopped right at his mouth. He was smelling the meat, choking on his own saliva and he died. He was a bad person."

"What would you do in his shoes?"

"I would have thrown the meat on the floor and waited for the guards. The guards would have killed us and given him the meat. The saliva from the smell of meat would not have choked him. I never wanted to be the prisoner in charge of the cell. I was entitled to one piece of meat, and he could have three. If he weren't so dumb, someone could have pressed a certain point behind the ear of each of his enemies. They would have fallen asleep, and he would have to share the meat with just one man."

"You said *someone*. You were the only one in that cell who knew which points to press?"

"Yes, I was. These silly people, they think just because I quarreled with Ho Chi Min, I stopped being a soldier of the revolution?"

"Have you killed anyone in your cell?"

"No. I sat in the corner by the door. I was entitled to one piece of meat, but I gave it to someone else. While they were busy dividing the meat, I split."

"You escaped from prison?"

"I did. You asked about the helicopter. I never got on that helicopter."

"Tell me more. Would you like some more beer?"

"Yes, I would. Beer is like bread."

"So true. Hien, I knew people in Russia who drank only beer and ate just a little dried fish or sunflower seeds and subsisted on that."

"You have smart friends. Beer is like bread. A man cannot live without beer, or bread, or rice. So, I fled. I fled from prison. It was really bad there. I liked the Americans. Everyone ran towards the helicopter, and I ran in the other direction."

"Tell me more."

Hien smiles. He knows that it's customary for the host to speak before the guest. He also knows that a polite man would always listen to someone more than twice his age.

"Everyone ran for the helicopter, and I ran into the jungle. Ho Chi Min betrayed me, and I was imprisoned. I escaped from prison and managed to reach the USSR. Things were good in USSR. But then Gorbachev came to power, and things turned bad again. Nobody was interested in protecting me. I went to the KGB, and they had no idea who I was. They said that Ho Chi Min is long dead, and I am of no interest to them. They said, "Go back to your country, go back to Vietnam." You're right. I would have been killed before the plane touched down in Hanoi."

"Hien, tell me about the Americans. I read a book by this one American about how he fought in the Vietnam war. He manned a machine gun, and the Vietnamese just kept coming. Row after row, he gunned them down, and row after row, they kept coming. He went crazy. Many people went crazy there. He writes that even now, many years later, whenever he closes his eyes, he sees rows of Vietnamese coming and hears the rattle of the machine gun."

"These weren't Vietnamese. The Vietnamese are smart; they hid in the trees and aimed well."

"Could they have been Chinese?"

"Maybe. I don't give a damn. Americans are good guys. The Chinese wanted to make Chinese out of us. The French wanted to make French out of us. The Americans wanted nothing of the kind. Remember this simple formula. Rice first, books in Vietnamese second, meat third. The Americans had nothing against any of these things."

"What happened then?"

"The Vietnamese state security sent two boys after me. The boys had knives. I walked slowly, and they followed me. I led them to the phone booth. Then I called and summoned an ambulance for them."

"They just stood there watching you make a phone call?"

"They didn't stand. They were withering on the ground and wailing in pain. That's what happens when one's knees and elbows are twisted out of their sockets."

"You maimed them?"

"Any doctor would be able to reset these dislocated joints. I am what you call *Spetznaz* in Russian -- did I say it right?"

"Yes, you are *Spetznaz*. And you are seventy-two years old. Hien, did the government of Vietnam authorize the publication of my book?"

"No. I will copy the book onto very fine rice paper. All the comrades in Vietnam will read it. Everyone who reads it will make two other copies by hand."

"Will they let you?"

"Of course. Sooner or later, they will. We know how to wait."

Bull

Corrida. A Spanish tradition. I respect traditions. Nobody should prohibit traditions. It's impossible to prohibit traditions, and that is good. If Spain outlaws corrida, nothing will change. Outside people will comply with the law, but inside they will remain the same. They are people, after all. If corrida is outlawed, they will still have soccer. There will always be crowded stadiums, loud screams, and a thirst for a spectacle. I have nothing against corrida or soccer. I am against prohibitions. I don't like an electrified crowd. I don't like loud screaming from a thousand mouths in unison.

Corrida is quite simple entertainment. People put on beautiful clothes, take a piece of iron into their hands, and try to kill a bull. While one of the attempts to kill the bull, the others enjoy the spectacle. Everyone is entertained. The bull has to be killed beautifully and skillfully. The bull has to be killed well. Nobody feels sorry for the bull; the bull is just an animal. Nobody feels sorry for the people either. They are human. They had the good fortune to be born human, and therefore they can attend corrida. Why would someone feel sorry for someone who is fortunate?

I am a bull. Just like that. No explanation is needed. I am not a human. I wasn't fortunate enough to be born human. A human, too, is an animal, but a bipedal animal. I don't stand a chance to become bipedal. Regretting that you are no bipedal is silly. Dreaming of a life whose sole purpose is to walk on two legs is equally silly. I would have made a lousy ostrich. I don't want to be an ostrich or a penguin. So, a bull it is.

I didn't choose this. The people in suits and ties did. They chose for me a life and death of an animal. Even now, they sit in their theatre boxes and wait for me to die. Let them. I do not wish death on them in return. I don't wish death on anyone. I am not a human being. I am cruel as only an animal can be. I am only cruel at the moment of pain and despair. I will never reach the human point of being cruel just for the hell of it.

I don't like the sight of blood. I don't like the color red. I am a bull, after all.

A bull is not free to choose whether he lives or dies. The only thing he can chose is whether to be a good bull or a bad bull. In either case, he has to die.

A bad bull doesn't want to die. A bad bull enters the arena only because he is being poked by sharp pikes. A bad bull wishes to live. A bad bull doesn't feel like dying beautifully to entertain a bunch of men and women dressed in their Sunday best. The viewing public doesn't like the bad bull, and there is no thrill in killing him. No-one feels sorry for the bad bull. People regret only the time wasted on him, the grass he ate, and the sun that shined on him undeservingly. One feels sorry for the people who have to kill the bad bull. At the moment they kill a bad bull, they resemble monkeys a little too closely for comfort.

After corrida, people cut the bull to pieces and eat him. They don't do it because they are hungry. From a purely gastronomical standpoint, a bull killed in a corrida fight is not very valuable. In order to obtain tender, tasty meat, a bull needs to be castrated. But they eat anyway. They eat a publicly killed bull to demonstrate just how male they are. On the plate, a piece of the dead bull looks the same as a piece of the dead cow. No-one feels sorry for a bull on the plate, or the cow, for that matter.

I observe. I put together the world like a puzzle. I don't give a damn about their knives and pikes. I don't give a damn about the fact that there is one of me and lots of them. I didn't choose. I really wanted to live like a human being. I wanted to live among people and die like a human being. Even if I am a bull. Even if I am a bull, I didn't want to die in the arena. Even if I am a bull, I would have preferred to die in a fight with someone whose strength equals mine. Let them cut me to pieces. Let the well-dressed monkeys dance their celebratory dance around me. Let them. They can't behave any other way and will never learn. They are people, after all.

This is not a real fight. The script is pre-written. The tables are set, and I will be eaten. But I will try. I will not give up trying. If fortune smiles at me, I will swipe one of them with my horn. I will kill him. I do not wish for anyone's death, but if death is their wish—so be it. If they so desire to see blood—fine, but it will not be just my blood. Let him die along with me. Unlike me, he actually had a choice, and he chose this profession. I can do it. I hope I can. I am a good bull.

Little Boxes

American "little boxes"—a collection of neat suburban homes that all look alike and house like-minded people. America's answer to racism. In my entire life, I have not collected enough letters and enough words to tell this story. Racism is seen as a way to separate people and a reason to hate people of a different race. The little boxes also separate people and place them each behind his own wall, into a box devoid of anything unique. Very few can look at them and see the beauty of racial diversity—a beauty attractive and frightening all at once, a beauty that forces one to look at oneself and others and admit the differences in skin color, place of birth, and education.

I am Latin American. I have a Latin American appearance. There is nothing good or bad about it. There is nothing good when you learn that a slight kink in your hair reveals your African origins as well.

I am a fiery cocktail of several races, mixed in one individual. I was born non-Russian, and that is not the same as being born Russian. No-one except Russians understand me when I say I was born non-Russian. Except for Russians and fellow non-Russians. I am entitled. I am entitled to talk about Russians and non-Russians. I am a Russian. Or a non-Russian. It's irrelevant one way or another.

It won't be easy to explain, but I will give it a good old elementary school try. Ever since I remember myself, I was learning the Russian language. Best in my class, best in my school, one of the best literary "users" of the Russian language—that's me, forever Russian and equally forever non-Russian. A laureate of the Russian Booker Prize, the most Russian of Russians—olive skin, aquiline nose, black hair in tight curls, dark brown eyes with the unusually bright white sclera. For some reason, it's my eyes that racists find most offensive. To me, they are just eyes, but their color sure makes some people angry.

It's not like I am dying to change my appearance. If only I had one working arm, or two. If only I could squeeze someone's throat, the color of my eyes would suddenly become a non-issue. And a silly proud dream of having a gun, a simple Colt, carries me into the world where I can take on the blue-eyed blonde elite in a fair fight.

That racism, familiar and straightforward, without a veneer of civilization is much more understandable and comfortable to me than the refined, subtle racism of old Europe. Russian racism is simpler and more honest than its European counterpart. But even European racism doesn't get close to American racism.

———— ◆ ————

A girl. A typical Latina. My wheelchair quickly rolls up to the bureaucratic window behind which she sits.

"Do you mind if a non-native English speaker handles your inquiry?"

I don't mind. I don't mind at all. In a country where almost a third of the population speaks Spanish as their first language, "non-native English speaker" is just a lot of words for "Spanish speaker." The girl rises slightly from her chair to have a good look at me.

"You are in a wheelchair. Usually, these issues take up to a month, but I will see what I can do in your case. Have a good day."

Exactly a week later, my documents come to me via courier. The courier is a slight youth with coffee-colored skin and brown eyes.

"Sign here and here. Good luck to you."

Of course, I will always have good luck from now on. I am, after all, Latin American.

———— ◆ ————

Supermarket. A large supermarket. Everything is friendly and accessible. I can talk to the manager and ask for someone on the supermarket staff to help me.

"Would you mind if a non-native English speaker helps you?"

"Not at all. Jorge and I got along just fine last time."

We stroll around the supermarket. I follow Jorge's lead.

"You like these tomatoes, Jorge? If you were shopping, which tomatoes would you buy?"

"None. These tomatoes here are impossible to eat."

"I lived in Spain, Jorge, and you in Mexico. Both of us can't pass the fish department without laughing."

Jorge smiles. Like me, he understands that the fish department has no business smelling like fish. In Mexico and in Spain, fish is sold fresh. We load the shopping cart according to my list.

"Hi, how are you?"—a female cashier greets me.

"Fine"—I reply—"I could have been better, but not to complain."

"Listen, Ruben, my girlfriend wants to move to Spain. What would you tell her?"

"I would tell her to forget about doing something that stupid."

"But she thinks things will be easier for her there. Everyone there speaks Spanish."

"That's the point"—I reply—"That's the whole point. She would never be able to get a job in the supermarket. Only Spaniards work in supermarkets. There are no jobs, and the jobs that exist go to the natives. Here you are a nobody, and in Spain, you will be worse—a competitor. Here you are paid enough money to rent a place of your own. In Spain, your friend would have to board with a family. And one more thing. The only job your friend can count on in Spain is being a domestic. Being a domestic is much harder in Spain than in the USA."

I pay for my purchase, and the woman discusses my words with the other cashiers. I understand every word. I am, after all, Latin American.

Rina and I are renting an apartment in a housing complex. Centralized service, centralized repairs, a centralized mess. One of the two toilets in our apartment clogged. It happens. My wife is at work all day and talking to the plumber falls on me. He quickly enters and is about to leave quickly.

"You have two toilets in the apartment. This isn't an emergency issue."

I realize that the plumber doesn't have much love for his superiors or his clients. The only ones who benefit from his work are the owners of the housing complex. He sincerely doesn't understand why these gringo men can't repair their own toilets. There are no tips, not even for emergencies in the middle of the night. The Residents' Information Booklet states explicitly that the housing complex staff is prohibited from accepting tips from residents. In my case, things are more complicated—it is kind of apparent by looking at me why I can't repair my own toilet. My skin color and my kinky hair reveal by non-White origins. I can see that the man hesitates. I understand him; I know what it means—to lose a job.

"Please"—I tell him—"The toilet that works is inaccessible by wheelchair."

"You speak Spanish."

He hears the Spanish language and his idea of how things are in the world undergoes a transformation.

"Wait"—I say—"I have a gift for you."

"We are prohibited from taking money from residents."

"It's not money. What is your name?"

"Jose."

"Jose, please take a book off the shelf. It is my book. I wrote it. I am a writer."

We speak Spanish to each other. We speak Spanish, and this erases the boundary between a plumber and a client.

The Spanish language has a formal "you" and an informal "you." In Spain, the formal "you" is hardly ever used. While I strain to remember how to say the formal "you" in Latin American Spanish, Jose resolves this question for me. He addresses me with an informal "you," and that makes me very happy.

"Just because you wrote a book, it does not make you a writer. How about I test you?"

"It's impossible. How will you know if I am a writer or not?"

"Easy. Who is Gabriel Garcia Marquez?"

"A famous Colombian writer. He wrote *Nadie le escribe al coronel, Cien años de aislamiento,* and *Otoño del Patriarca.*"[1]

Jose stares in space. He thinks hard.

"You named these books correctly, but it was like you translated these names back to Spanish. You read them in a language other than Spanish?"

"I did."

"What language?"

"Russian."

"Russians are good people. Where did you learn Spanish?"

"In Madrid."

---

[1] No One Writes to the Colonel (El coronel no tiene quien le escriba), One Hundred Years of Solitude (Cien años de soledad), The Autumn of the Patriarch (El otoño del patriarca)

Suddenly Jose's eyes well up with tears.

"I will fix everything, don't you worry. I will replace everything I can replace with something newer and better. They buy the cheapest parts. The parts are cheap, and we don't cost them anything. We are on fixed salaries. Besides—I can see that Jose is about to start sobbing—They don't even know their own writers, let alone Marquez."

I am quiet. We both understand who "they" are.

Jose takes another look at my book.

"Thank you, I will read it."

I am alright. I have read many books. I am not a gringo. I am Latin American.

School

We came to the school. It was a very good Israeli school. Not just a good school, there are plenty of those around the world. This was the best of the best. None better. The atmosphere is calm and peaceful. If you invite a random person off the street to this school, he will get scared, and that's the best-case scenario. He will run away as fast as he can and never return to our school. But you and I are not random people. We found ourselves in a fairy tale. Modern electric wheelchairs, calm and joyful faces of the children. And the teachers' faces—calm and concentrated. Random teachers never make it to this school. Random people have no business being there at all.

Two boys gave a speech welcoming the first-grade class. The boys had a difficult time reading the notes, but they tried their best. Half an hour would be enough for a healthy high school kid to prepare a two-minute speech. These guys prepared for this moment for the last ten years. A little more than ten years of painstaking work, sleepless nights, victories, defeats, hopes, and disappointments. But how much these two minutes weigh on the scales of Eternity? Which multi-volume edition could possibly outweigh this half a page of text?

We, you, and I, attended very different schools.

We knew different teachers.

We knew that at this school, the best school in the world, Sophia will not have bad teachers.

I bought you ice cream. You walked along the street and sobbed, and I just could not calm you down.

I didn't sob. More than anything, I wished I could have attended this school as a child. I did not cry. Boys don't cry.

Fish

Sea. This is my sea. Sea cannot possibly belong to one man. Sea cannot be bought. But today, it belongs to me: such a mysterious and inexplicable phenomenon—the sea.

The sea is visible from the window of my apartment. Another sea. That one is also mine. I have three seas. Not many, but enough. For me—that's enough.

I squeeze the breathing tube with my teeth. "You will have everything I have"—I suddenly remember you said that. A fish swims by me. It's big and beautiful. The fish is also mine, but only for one second. The fish and I are on equal footing. I see him, and he sees me.

Up to that moment, I saw fish only in aquariums. That didn't seem fair. I am free, and the fish is inside a confined space. Of course, the aquarium has everything a fish needs to live—the oxygen filter works like clockwork, the food comes regularly and in abundance. Everything is nice in the aquarium, except there is no freedom. Maybe the fish in the aquarium is happy. Anything is possible. Every aquarium owner will say that the fish is happy in the aquarium. But I am not an aquarium owner. I believe that it's better for the fish to be free. I believe that it's better for me to be free.

Good-bye, fish! We will meet again. I am more than sure of it. No ifs or maybes. You are a beautiful fish; I like you. I will come to visit you again.

9th of AV

Bad days happen sometimes. Peaceful and joyful days happen sometimes. On the 8th of the Hebrew month of Av, the air conditioner broke down in our apartment. My daughter cries and fusses and refuses to go to bed. My wife does the best she can under the circumstances. Several times Rina takes Sophia to take a shower to cool down. We wake up tired and broken down in the morning. "What should I do?"—Rina asks. "Go to work"—I reply—"Every person is needed in his or her place."

Polina has a horrific pain attack. Polina wheels me into the bathroom, washes me, and sits me in the wheelchair. Polina almost collapses onto the couch; she is sitting and panting heavily. She cannot remain in a place with no air conditioner. "You are tired, go home. I will stay with Ruben,"—Michael tells her. Michael walks Polina to the bus stop. I, too, am out of sorts. My lungs are weak; I didn't have any sleep last night, as strong medicines in my body helped me overcome the heat and stuffy air.

I stay behind with Michael. From time to time, my vision becomes so clouded that I barely see his face. I really am in pain, in a lot of pain. I try to participate in the conversation, but I just had strong painkillers, and Michael had his dose of Ritalin. Michael keeps talking and talking. He always tells me everything he knows on any given subject. I shouldn't stop him. I should just listen and listen. This time Michael gives me a rundown on the mechanics of medieval armor.

The AC technician comes. Michael speaks to him in a language I don't understand. I will learn Hebrew; I sure as hell will. The AC technician leaves and comes back. The air conditioner is working.

Michael keeps talking to the AC technician. They speak about their service in the army. Nothing special. Yes, the AC technician was wounded in action. Yes, several bullets hit his body. Michael talks of his army service. It doesn't sound like anything special, but I know Michael well. Sometimes he lets things slip. Usually, he makes it sound like army service is nothing but a string of entertainments, theater excursions, and boat trips. He speaks about the theatre a lot, but when he speaks of actual service, he thinks hard before each word leaves his mouth. The AC technician understands. Both of them are forbidden from discussing their service at length. They just exchanged a couple of words, and that's enough.

The AC technician casts a quick glance at the photograph on my desktop. "*Isha sheli*"—I say—"Iraq."

I show the AC technician my books. His eyes fix on a large white book. It is my book. I wrote it. I am proud of it. The AC technician's fingers touch the raised Braille font. His grandfather couldn't see, and there were a lot of such books in their house. I tell him that the book was written in Esperanto. We laugh.

"You are a writer,"—says the AC technician and carefully places the book back on the shelf.

I tell him about Rina, about how she exchanged being a lawyer in the US for being a welder in Israel for the sake of our daughter. Michael translates. I say that I am thrilled that the technician repaired my AC on such a special day, the 9th of Av. I thank the technician. Michael translates. The technician gives me a good look; he sees my twisted body, my compressed chest, and understands that I risk landing in the hospital without AC.

Rina too could not talk about her work. In the US, she held a Top-Secret security clearance.

I am the only one who never held any kind of security clearance.

The AC technician leaves. Too bad. I want to talk with him like Michael does, easily and confidently. I regret not serving in the army.

Michael doesn't eat. I, too, refuse food at first. I want to be like Michael. I want to be with people who don't eat on the 9th of Av.

Michael boils some pasta. He then drains the pasta and bakes it in a pan with lots of eggs mixed in. This is called *kugel yerushalmi*. I need to eat. My medicines are powerful. Michael doesn't tell me this; he just places the plate in front of me.

We are silent.

At night Rina will come from work, tired and happy that she has me to come home to. Rina will dice some cucumbers, radishes, and hard-boiled eggs into a bowl and pour kefir over this. We call this dish *okroshka*. Rina is the only woman on a crew of twenty or so men. Rina operates a crane to move parts of a steel frame that will support a new airport being built in the Negev desert. "Every person is needed in his or her place,"—I repeat.

Every person is needed in his or her place.

Pacifist

Pacifist. All my life, I considered myself a pacifist. I never wanted to handle a weapon. I never wanted to kill people.

I never thought that having lived more than half of my earthly life, I would dream of serving in the army. Geographically Israel is a tiny country. An oasis of European hi-tech where Africa and Asia meet. Israel cannot afford to send its boys and girls to die overseas. Israel Defense Forces is truly an army of defense.

I am convinced that the IDF would do just fine without me. Israel has enough soldiers to protect itself from enemies. But Israel's army is not just about protection from enemies. In Israel, the army is the best way to make lifelong friends. The army is one of the best Hebrew teachers. The army is the future. The army is everything.

I was late. When I came here, I was too old for the army. Too late.

Yet, despite the "too late," I will hope and wait. I wait to be summoned. I will wait for the moment when the army finds something important for me to do.

I will wait.

Why I do not go

In recent times many people have reached to me with invitations to come to Russia. It's clear why they would like me to come to Russia. I can speak fluent Russian; I am a laureate, and all that jazz. The fact that I am disabled is invariably mentioned among my positive attributes. The disabled are supposed to help each other, and disability advocacy organizations are supposed to help the disabled. Most of the invitations come from disability advocacy organizations.

Sometimes people rebuke me for withdrawing from the human rights struggle in Russia, for forgetting about my homeland, and accuse me of things I had no idea of even while I lived in Russia, let alone now, after many years of living abroad.

I will respond to these rebukes in an orderly fashion, one by one.

I never forgot my homeland, even though the homeland periodically forgot me. While I lived in Russia, nobody invited me to speak at any event or to any kind of a public function. The only people they invited to those functions were well-fed invalids from Western countries in expensive wheelchairs, whose experience would not have helped me one bit because it was far from my reality as Jupiter is from Mars. Now I am the well-fed Western invalid in an expensive wheelchair whose experience is about as useful to Russian invalids as a fifth leg to a dog, or a fifth wheel to a cart or any other colorful metaphor you might like. The Russian language is rich in colorful metaphors.

But everything above is just lyrical stuff. Let's get down to more earthly business.

First, I am not well. I am not well to the point that I can require medical intervention at any given moment. The medical intervention itself is usually not complicated and can be accomplished at any clinic or hospital with expertise in geriatric or cardiac patients. Even a large hospital that has experience treating paralyzed individuals would suffice. Unfortunately, clinics and hospitals on such a level do not exist in Russia. This is not an attack on Russia; it is just a statement of an unfortunate fact. Russia has excellent doctors, but inferior medical technology and equipment. In order for me to take a trip to Russia, I would have to have a comprehensive medical insurance that would allow me to be transported for treatment to Finland, for example.

Second. My wheelchair costs a lot of money. Let us not forget that without the wheelchair, I lose the ability to work.

Third. Even if I have insurance and a wheelchair is insured, I will have to fly first class since I cannot sit in a regular airplane chair; in fact, I cannot sit in a regular chair at all. Plus, lodging in a hotel where facilities allow wheelchair access, and the services of an attendant will have to be paid for if I am to be invited.

Coming back to the lyrical stuff. Without these expenses, my trip to Russia cannot happen. But if this kind of money is available to be spent, it would be much more humane, logical, and effective to spend it on helping the disabled people who are trying to survive and live in Russia. The disabled people living in Russia are the true heroes; they are the ones that should be invited to sit on panels and speak at events.

There is no real work for me in Russia, and the last thing I want to be is a token invalid.

A little addendum. But Ed Roberts came to Russia. Correct. Ed Roberts came to Russia, and maybe I will come to Russia as well one day. I am no more and no less afraid for my life than Ed was. I will come when I feel that I really needed, needed for real work, not to entertain the public.

In my humble opinion, I can do enough for Russia right where I am, and I do just that. My articles and books are published in Russia, Russian specialists consult with me, and my friends who live in Russia know that I am always here for them. Despite the distance, despite my physical limitations.

Morning

Morning. Today I am having a good morning. Today I can sit down and write a book. I can calmly and confidently eat a plate of soup. I can give a public lecture. I can do everything. People will smile at me. People like good stories and happy endings. That's understandable. In this crazy life of ours, it is important to believe that things will turn out for the better. If this bespectacled guy in a wheelchair is in a good mood, every person on the planet has a chance of being in a good mood. At least everyone has a right to.

The people around me do not have the need to know about yesterday's details. Yesterday you gave me medicine. Yesterday I was in so much pain I was bouncing off walls. You gave me medicine, and you massaged my body, twisted into a knot of pain. You did a little more than impossible. And I? What could I do? I didn't want to take these medicines. The body refused to pay attention to the medicine or to your strong hands. Only after a while, things started working. Yesterday became today. I am fine. An excellent orator, a handsome middle-aged man. Almost nothing hurts me. I am fine.

I am rarely that fine. Behind my "fine," there is always the "bad" you and I shared and went through together. We will tell everyone how we overcame yesterday's "bad" together. Of course, we will.

Children

Euphoria. The first stage of immigration. You like everything. Everything is exciting; everything is interesting. I look around. Again, and again, I look around to see as much as I possibly can.

Children, lots of children. I have never seen so many healthy children. Where I came from, children are driven around in big yellow buses. Adults are also driven around on buses, but not all of them. I have seen enough adults. Adults decided to walk on the streets, but it could also be that these adults cannot afford their own personal little bus. I don't know. Anyway, every adult is supposed to have a car.

Each adult travels to work every day in his own little box. Every day adults return from work to eat, sleep, and exchange the false comfort of a big car for the true comfort of a small house.

Children are everywhere here. Children play on the streets, shout, and sing. Children are not hidden and locked away from the world of adults.

A boy squatted next to me. He is busy. The blazing Israeli sun shines through the lens in the boy's hand. The boy is trying to set fire to the end of his shoelace. I amble around the street. I take my sweet time. I have time. The boy has much more time than me. Smoke began rising from the shoelace. The boy rose and walked away. He doesn't need to rush. The boy has eternity.

Eternal Guest

They were playing backgammon. I could have expected anything, but not even the wildest of fantasies featured them playing backgammon. The waitress brought us delicious eggs, fried sunny side up, sausages, and beer. A regular diner, just a regular diner. People conversed, some were eating, and everyone drank the tastiest beer in the world. Czech beer. Feel free to challenge me on this last point. Germany has decent beer as well. German beer is actually very good. But I didn't try German beer until much later when I was in Germany. Nothing special. Beer is beer. It was in the Czech Republic, where I tried beer for the first time in my life. Everything beautiful happens for the first time. When the waitress said, "boys, can you please close the door behind yourselves, the draft is coming from the outside,"—I was beyond surprised. I have just witnessed a miracle. The boys politely thanked the waitress and closed the door behind themselves. They also played chess in that diner. Chess is too much. Chess is a luxury, but they played and drank beer. I wanted to stay in this country where I have witnessed so many miracles for the first time. Before, I only saw these types of things on TV. It's just a diner in a small, poor country. The Czech Republic. It was in the Czech Republic where someone apologized to me for the first time, apologized for the fact that the movie theatre didn't have a working elevator. For the first time, I was a guest in someone else's country. Everything in the Czech Republic was for the first time for me. I met Aurora in the Czech Republic. The Czech Republic is a small country, and I realized that they could not afford a paralyzed man. Fine. I am not angry; I understand.

Spain is a tiny country. According to all national and international law, I am Spanish. I have a Spanish passport. Spain is a good country. A small country, smaller than the Czech Republic. In Spain, I became a well-known writer. In Spain, I was invited to upscale restaurants. Sometimes I glimpsed the restaurant bills, and the price tag of Spanish hospitality began to dawn on me. Spain is also a very small and very poor country. In Spain, I had a room, a window, a kitchen. Everything was beautiful in my Spain. Even the view from the window was beautiful. Even the door handle, even the crack on the wall across from my desk, even a portable AC unit stuffed with straw. The Spanish took my books to heart; they are legitimately proud of the Spanish writer Ruben Gallego. Spain will forever remain in my soul. The Spanish are kind, hospitable people. I like the Spanish. I learned the language; I grew to appreciate olive oil; I looked deep inside the Spanish soul. I like the picaresque novel as an art form, but I didn't particularly appreciate living inside the picaresque novel. I didn't like the idea of running away from the police and confusing my tracks. Anyway, it's kind of hard to be an illegal alien when you are in a wheelchair. The kind and intelligent Spanish asked me to pay for citizenship. They asked me to get rich quickly. If I were a rich man, they would have forgiven everything, even my disability. If I paid up, I could count on a place under the sun. Even bandits and murderers fleeing from their home countries' authorities can remain in Spain as long as they pay up.

Russia is a small country. Really small country, less than the Czech Republic. Russia is a great small country. Russians don't drink. They really don't. Maybe, when they are in the mood. Russians work and study. They teach children and treat patients; they build houses and plant gardens. They do all that when there are jobs. When there are jobs and hope for the children's better future. Russians drink from hopelessness and despair. They drink to cope with grief. Russian barbaric customs seem cruel only at first glance. The honesty and directness of the Russian people are not tainted with refined civilized cruelty. They just leave the weak and the helpless to die alone. It's hard for a disabled person to survive among the Russians. The Spanish left a disabled child to the Russians to care for. The Russians treated the young hostage like one of their own. I ate the same food Russian children eat. I read the same books Russian children read. I suffered from the same diseases. I crawled on the same snow. I became more Russian than Russians themselves. I became a Russian writer. Russians don't kill writers, not anymore. When I wrote books, I wrote for the Russians. I knew it was possible to kill a writer in Russia, but a writer has a chance to survive. So be it. Spain likes its writers. It is as difficult to kill a writer in Spain as in Russia. The Spanish and the Russians are alike. Too much alike.

Germany is a great country. In Germany, I was a nobody. I came to this country a nobody, and I left a nobody. Everything is logical. Why on earth would a holder of a Spanish passport live in Germany? Germany is a small country, smaller than Spain. The difference between them is not that great. In Germany, I had a fireplace. I like watching wood burn in the fireplace. I like looking at fire burn. The door to the street in Germany was different from the Spanish door. The German door was sturdier and better made.

Sometimes I was invited places. Everyone wanted to extend an invitation to a famous writer. The kind Spanish welcomed me as a VIP guest. The excitable Italians wanted to see and hear me again and again. I am very much loved in Italy.

The stern Vikings—the Swedes and the Norwegians -- showed me their countries' greatness in their usual reserved and severe manner. Museums, theatres, hockey. Restaurants and small diners hosted me with severe dignity. Everything was delicious and fresh. The Norwegians are more hospitable than the Spanish are. Modestly and honestly, the Norwegians collected money for me. The Norwegians helped me when no-one else could or would. I respect Norway.

America—the faraway enchanted country, the pinnacle of dreams and hopes of millions. America—the dream stretching from sea to shining sea, turned out to be regular US of A. I had nothing to offer this great country. The USA is a big country. Everything is big here. In the US, I could ride around the streets in the American-made wheelchair, look at people rushing to work, wander around the streets of the capital. That's it. Everything else cost money. Nothing interesting. When a crisis hit, unknown Russian people sent me money and words of support. I respect Russians. They are noble and cruel. Russians don't drink. They don't drink at all. But I am confident that when I was about to depart this life, in Russia and beyond its borders, thousands of Russian speakers raised a glass of vodka or a cup of tea to my health.

And then I grew tired, like any other man would towards the end of his life. I grew tired of counting money and converting every human action to a dollar value. I realized that the Americans are good guys, but not my cup of tea. And when I realized this, I left this concentrated paradise. I went to a place where I could die in peace.

I wanted to die by the sea. I've never seen the sea. I never saw the ocean swallow the setting sun. Israel is a huge country, bigger than America. I wanted to see the sea before I died.

In Israel, I was welcomed as an honored guest. In Israel, there was a place at the table for me. I was offered the most delicious meat and the most exquisite Israeli wine. The local craftsman put together the best wheelchair in the world—for me. My American wife got offered the best job, and my daughter enrolled in the best school. I realized that none of this is going to last forever. In the years of wandering, I got used to the idea that I will always be a guest, no matter where I go. Sooner or later, a guest leaves, taking beautiful memories with him. Sooner or later, a guest gets up even from the most hospitable table.

We are all guests in this world. But I am a special guest. My time in this world is over; it's time to leave. The small flag on a chess clock almost fell. My time was almost up. I spoke Spanish to the Israeli anesthesiologist, but what does that matter in a country of a hundred languages. As he was adjusting the mask to my face, I managed to ask him, "How much time do I have left?" And then I fell asleep. Six months have passed. Six months is time enough to realize that the Israeli doctors accomplished the impossible. In six months, it became clear that the very question "how much time do I have left?" lost its meaning. I will remain a guest in this boundless and beautiful country. I am a guest. An eternal guest.

Bread

Bakery. A regular bakery. People go in and out. It's Friday afternoon. I stand outside and observe. I like observing. I like the people. I like the scent of freshly baked bread.

A dad and a little daughter. Dad is in a good mood. The dad's skin tone is about the same as mine. Dad buys bread. Dad buys lots of bread. The daughter tells dad something. I don't know their language, but somehow, I understand. Dad buys a small bread roll for his daughter. The little girl says something in Hebrew and that I understand. She is blessing the bread.

The owner of the bakery walks out the door. He approaches me confidently. We try to figure out in which language to converse. I try, and so does my vis-à-vis. He speaks Arabic, Farsi, and some other languages I have no clue about.

A man enters the bakery. He is dressed very modestly in all black, but his clothes are impeccably clean. He takes the bread and leaves.

Hebrew. The baker and I are left to make do with Hebrew.

"I am not alone"—I tell the baker—"I arrived in Israel just recently."

"But you will have bread for Shabbat?"

"Of course, I will."

"You don't live alone?"

"I live with my wife and daughter."

The man who bakes bread gives me a joyful look.

I am not alone. I will have bread for Shabbat.

I will always have bread for Shabbat.

I Regret Nothing

All my life, I dreamt of walking. I never learned to walk. But it wasn't for the sake of walking that I wanted to walk. I wanted to run. I dreamt of not just running; I dreamt of beating everyone else in the race. Having legs for only a portion of your life is enough. Having legs in childhood and youth is enough. It's wonderful to have arms and legs and receive a university diploma, a driver's license, or any other piece of paper that proves you are a human being.

What happens, after that point, doesn't matter. You already proved yourself. If you invest enough in your future, you will remain like everyone else, even if in that future you find yourself in a wheelchair or on crutches. You will be like healthy people. That would have been enough for me, more than enough. By age thirty, I could have been a famous astrophysicist. Not bad. Many would have been happy to become astrophysicists. A wheelchair is a setback. A wheelchair is a major setback. Nobody would want to find themselves in a wheelchair. But being an astrophysicist in a wheelchair is much better than just being in a wheelchair.

Great athletes and great actors can also find themselves in a wheelchair. That's particularly awful—to find yourself in a wheelchair when you spend your life showing people strong willpower and iron muscles. It is difficult; it is exceedingly difficult to spend your body's resources on not looking pitiful, to turn yourself inside out trying to claw a plate of standard food and a glass of milk out of life. A theatre actor has it harder. The actor must turn his very soul inside out, to prove his right to life with sweat and blood. The actor must prove he has a right to live, and the viewing public owes almost nothing. The viewing public gives the actor money. Money—small but serious tickets that give a man a right to live—doesn't come easy to the actor. Sometimes, on rare occasions, a theatre actor is invited to play in a movie. The movie industry, while it gives the actor money, sucks him into the devilish vortex of playing with death. The public always wants more; the public is always unhappy and complaining. They paid, after all. The actor lives his entire life on stage, not having anything he can call "personal." He has no privacy. The actor can lose it, drink an extra glass, pop an extra pill, shoot an extra dose up his veins. But the public wants more anyway. The more genuine suffering, the merrier. One more glass, one more pill, one more shot. Sometimes it seems like the public is right. Whether in a theatre or in the movies, the spectator paid his honest money. The spectator must give a performance at the job interview so that he can get a job. The spectator pays not only with his money but with his time.

Anyone can become disabled, not just astrophysicists. Very often, a man who becomes disabled discovers that now he is obligated to rejoice. Rejoice all the time, strongly and sincerely. And smile. Always smile; smile at everyone. Just like it was yesterday. If the man became disabled a year before, anything that occurred before that moment seems just like it was yesterday. Yesterday he worked and went on vacations. Yesterday he sped down a steep slope on mountain skis. Yesterday he grumbled against congested roads and exorbitant taxes. Yesterday he zipped his own fly, brewed his own tea, held a cup of tea to his own mouth, drank the tea by himself, and washed the glass after himself. And now—it's over. No more mountain skis, asshole bosses, or exorbitant taxes. The things that made up his life vanished. All he has left is a wheelchair and permission, almost a mandate, to be constantly joyful and smile. To smile broadly and sincerely.

I have it easier, much easier. Having lived half my lifetime, I am content with my lot. My piece of life is guaranteed to me. The Jewish surgeon carefully stitched my body together. He cut and stitched in such a way that my body works like a clock. My body stopped bothering me about dumb things. I feel pain and that, paradoxically, enables me to live longer. The ability to feel pain is really a boon to me and my doctors to continue the quest for keeping my body among the living. With my left hand, I confidently move my electric wheelchair around the street. I can see, and I can hear. It is enough, more than enough to feel genuine joy, not joy for show. I know that things could have been worse, a lot worse.

Slowly hitting the keys on the keyboard, I proved my strength to society and asked for my place in a silly hierarchy of human beings.

I have proven everything. I was ready to die, but now I will go on living.

While normal boys walked to school, I crawled in the snow. While normal boys slapped the carpet with their palms as a gesture of defeat in the game, I was envious of them, but I kept crawling. While good normal boys studied medicine or mathematics, I read anything that came my way. And I crawled. I kept crawling.

While boys who had no knowledge of what a prison is or what an orphanage is acquired estimable professions, I read. I read, and I crawled.

While good, intelligent, and diligent boys strove to make their mark on physics or medicine, I read.

While some men my age got their Nobel Prize or just a tenured professorship, I crawled and read. It's not that hard, crawling on the wooden floor, but suddenly I found myself crawling on the parquet. So, parquet it will be. Parquet turned to be wood, just plain old wood. It's not that hard—to crawl on wood.

Suddenly, without telling me, someone organized carpets for me, many carpets. My hands cannot be held as open palms or tightened into a fist. I tried; I honestly tried to slap the carpet with my palm, but in the world of art, integrity, and fair play, it proved elusive. My movements were not noticed; my words were not heard. Nobody cared whether or not I slapped the carpet. Time and again, I tried to prove that I was just another Russian actor. Just another actor, like so many before me.

I was praised; I was genuinely praised. I am not going to pretend it doesn't feel nice when people acknowledge my modest efforts. Everyone complimented me, but no-one dared acknowledge my rights to a bare minimum and enough medicine to sustain my body. No country in the world gave me asylum—bread and a little medicine. Nobody wanted a man whose place is in the nursing home. Everyone felt awkward once they realized that my descriptions of nursing homes and long-term care facilities in their countries would be strong and precise. Everyone was afraid to admit that old age and disability are nothing pleasant to look at in every corner of our planet.

I was praised, and every time I made another lunge forward, someone put a carpet underneath. Crawling on the carpet is difficult, but I crawled. I crawled and read, I crawled and read.

And then. And then my books were quoted in every corner of the universe. Then the artificial carpet turned into natural beach sand. When I met Polina, I had to crawl on the sand a little more. I crawled on the sand, knowing what will happen next. The caring hands of the citizens of a uniquely great country lifted me and carried me. I swam in the sea, and it was not a dream. I rode on the waves of one of the three great seas of a great country.

Very long ago, I lost the habit of comparing myself to other actors in this universal theater. Very long ago, I decided that I will not have an old age—the disabled don't live that long. I thought it was kind of dumb to expect a mangled body to last the same amount of time as a healthy body. I was wrong. I was mistaken. The Jewish surgeon proved me wrong. I lived to be fifty, but I know that's not the end; 'til one hundred and twenty. In this country, everyone wishes everyone else to live 'til one hundred and twenty.

I don't regret; I regret nothing about the life I lived. I can see the sea from the windows of my home. Every evening I am privileged to see the hot Middle Eastern sun fall into the ocean. Every morning I withstand pain. That's not so bad. I can live with my mangled body. It's not worth regretting that at birth, I was unfortunate. I know, I am absolutely sure that every day someone discovers me for themselves. Not exactly me, not all of me, but a cast of me, an imprint of me—my book. Time and again, I am needed by someone. That's the main thing, to be needed. That's the main thing in life.

The Inuit Character Act

Somewhere far, far away, all the way up to the Arctic live a people called the Inuit. They know they are the Inuit. But others call them "representatives of the Arctic indigenous population." Nobody asked the Inuit themselves if they wish to be called this. But serious men wearing serious suits and warming their serious body parts in official chairs in the most important organization in the world decided to call the Inuit just that.

If you live in the Arctic, you live rather simply. When the ice cracks under the sled, you have two minutes for everything—to pull the sled from under the ice and change into dry clothes. If you managed to do that in two minutes, you are an Inuit. If you failed, you are a representative of the Arctic indigenous population. Serious men in serious suits sit on serious money and think of you. I am not against it; let them think. But two minutes is two minutes. You can accomplish a lot in two minutes, like pull your sled from under the ice and change into dry clothes. Instead of this nonsense, you can get busy reading the chairman's report, the vice-chairman's report, the committee chairman's report, the committee vice-chairman's report, the special working group chairman's report, the special working group vice-chairman's report. To be brief, you can't drive around in a sled with all these reports. Every gram of unnecessary weight pushes the sled closer to the abyss. Something tells me that out of all our civilization has to offer, the Inuit have the most use for a Ziploc bag. You can put a box of matches in a Ziploc bag. If you have a box of matches wrapped tightly in a Ziploc bag, you are a happy, joyful, confident, and strong Inuit. If an Inuit agrees to put on a serious black suit and sit in a chairman's warm chair, he is no longer Inuit; he is a civilized representative of the Arctic indigenous population. There are few real Inuit, but they exist. I don't know how many committee members are out there, but they don't interest me. They are not capable of building a fire in two minutes and changing into dry clothes. They cannot make this important decision without multiple consultations and securing multiple permissions.

About twice a week, some member of some committee or subcommittee issues a condemnation to my country. I am used to it, let them condemn, but sometimes I wonder why my country is the one that gets the most censure. The men in important chairs almost selflessly think of my future. Day and night, they think of how I should and should not live. But sometimes, this makes me feel awkward. Why am I worse than an Inuit? A couple of mouse clicks and I sigh with relief. These saintly people have thought not just of me, but of representatives of the indigenous population of the Arctic. I am not joking or telling yarns—there really is an official document telling the Inuit how they should live their lives. This priceless document allows the Inuit to fish and light a fire in the tundra. For decades, these saintly people waste trees and ink on the Inuit. The Inuit don't give a damn. Two minutes are all the Inuit have. Nobody is going to give the Inuit a warm chair and a nutritious dinner four times a day. It's just the Inuit and his two minutes—that is it. That is all that is needed for the survival of this strong and proud people.

From time to time, I am being fired upon. I have two minutes to reach a bomb shelter. But I am a devious man. I don't have to spend these two minutes because I sleep in the bomb shelter. In case of an emergency, my wife and daughter hide in my room. It is a well-built room with sturdy walls. When I am being fired upon, the representatives of my country and my army fire back. In most cases, they manage to intercept an enemy rocket before it even goes full speed. We violate human rights as often as possible. We violate them by lighting a match and changing into dry clothes. We have no time to read reports and resolutions by stern men in black suits. The resolutions are too long, but we want to remain alive right at this moment. I am not angry at these severe men in black suits. Let them sit and write. In theory, I must prove to them my right to exist, to explain to the community of the world that the rocket aimed for my home is flying right now. This year, this month, this day, this hour. We are not dumber than the Inuit; we realize that a man needs to survive first and prove things later. A genuine real Inuit would never read the nonsense written by people who never fell under the ice and never caught a single fish for their tribe's survival.

I am a writer, and I have a rich imagination. But not in the wildest of my nightmares, could I imagine a country, a society, or a single human being who agrees to run their lives according to recommendations from warm chairs. The chair has it fine, and the occupant of the chair has it even better. But what do I have to do with it? I have two minutes, and I am the one being fired at.

It's been almost a week since my country declared that it has a Jewish character. I object. I vehemently object to the idea of enshrining obvious things in law. We all know that there was nothing here except swamps and deserts before the Aliyah of the strong and intelligent people. Okay, I agree to admit that the Inuit built the railroads, schools, universities, and factories. If tomorrow announces that my country has an Inuit character, I will not object. I agree to give the Inuit the authority to judge my conduct and weigh my decisions. These brave people will take the same two minutes to realize what Jews already realize. If your life is in mortal danger, all you want is to light a fire and change to dry clothes. We are very much like the Inuit. We had six days to resolve the question what character our state will have. Six days is not a lot of time. No other people accomplished this—to unite, strike, and emerge victorious in six days. We had seventy years to learn that no country will sacrifice its soldiers for our survival. At best, they will send us another investigative commission. We don't want much. We don't agree to little. All we want is to survive. We have no time to read lofty words on white paper. We want to avoid being killed. And all we have is two minutes.

I am ready to call my country an Inuit country. The Inuit survive where no-one else can. We survive where no-one else wanted to survive before us.

Diplomacy. Fine, let's engage in diplomacy. But let this be a one-on-one diplomacy. We will make peace with everyone. We will talk to anyone who wants to talk and reach a solution. Soon, very soon, our small globe called Earth will erupt in waves of terror. We are ready. We are always ready. We have two minutes.

———— ◆ ————

ABOUT THE AUTHOR

Rubén David González Gallego is a Russian writer and journalist. Rubén was born in USSR without the use of his hands and feet. The official diagnosis is cerebral palsy. The Soviet officials have told his mother that the child has died and sent him to a state orphanage. Rubén spent his childhood in orphanages and nursing homes of the Soviet Union.

In 2001, when he was 33 years old, he met his mother for the first time at a conscious age. Rubén traveled around Europe and the world. He lived in the German Freiburg, Spanish Madrid. In the mid-2000s, he left for the United States.

He is an author of three books. In 2003 he received one of the most prestigious national literary awards, "Booker—Open Russia," for his first book, "White on Black." The second book, "Chess," was first published under the title "I am sitting on the shore." In 2019 this book won the Best European Book (Fiction) at the first-ever European Chess Award Ceremony.

Now Rubén, his wife, and daughter are living in Israel.

ABOUT THE AUTHOR

www.ingramcontent.com/pod-product-compliance
Lightning Source LLC
LaVergne TN
LVHW010626100826
845148LV00014B/3126

* 9 7 8 1 7 3 6 1 4 1 1 3 7 *